D1178816

INNOCENT SECRETARY...
ACCIDENTALLY
PREGNANT

INNOCENT SECRETARY... ACCIDENTALLY PREGNANT

BY

CAROL MARINELLI

First published in Great Britain 2009
Large Print edition 2010
Harlequin Mills & Boon Limited,
Eton House, 18-24 Paradise Road,
Richmond, Surrey TW9 1SR

© Carol Marinelli 2009

ISBN: 978 0 263 21207 5

Harlequin Mills & Boon policy is to use papers that are
natural, renewable and recyclable products and made
from wood grown in sustainable forests. The logging and
manufacturing process conform to the legal environmental
regulations of the country of origin.

Printed and bound in Great Britain
by CPI Antony Rowe, Chippenham, Wiltshire

For Beryl with love from Carol

xxx

CHAPTER ONE

EMMA *had* been honest—had even admitted during her telephone interview that she was attending night school on a Wednesday night and studying art and that in a couple of years she was hoping to pursue it full-time.

Everything had gone really well, until the second Evelyn had walked out to greet Emma—and Emma truly didn't understand why.

She'd prepared so carefully for the interview. Reading everything she could get her hands on about D'Amato Financiers—about their spectacular rise, even in gloomy times. Luca D'Amato had a no-nonsense attitude—there was no secret formula to his success, she had read in a rare interview he had given—just sound decisions and fiscal transparency and the refusal to be swayed by hype. Yes, she'd read up on him and then gone through her favourite glossy magazines and followed every last piece of advice in preparation for this afternoon.

Emma had scoured the second-hand shops and found a stunning—if just a touch tight for her well-rounded figure—pale lilac linen designer suit, had had her thick brown ringlets blowdried straight and smoothed up into a smart French roll, and, horribly broke, she had, on the afternoon of her interview, as one magazine had cheekily advised, gone to the make-up counter at a department store and pretended that she was a bride-to-be and trying out looks for her wedding day.

Her brothers had always teased her about her obsession with magazines and her father had moaned about how many she had bought, but they had been her lifeline. Growing up without a mother, living in a rough-and-tumble house that the little girls she'd invited to come over and play had never returned to, Emma had lived her childhood and teenage years reading the glossies for advice, about friends and bullying and boys. It was the magazines that had taught her about deodorant and kisses and bras. The magazines she had turned to when at twelve she had been teased for having hairy legs. And though her devotion to them had waned somewhat, at the ripe age of twenty-four it had been the magazines she had immediately turned to for make-up and grooming tips to land her dream job.

She looked fantastic, *just* the image she had been hoping to achieve—smart, sassy, groomed— exactly the right look for a modern working girl in the city.

Evelyn clearly didn't agree.

Her interviewer was dressed in a stern grey suit, with black flat shoes. Her fine blonde hair was cut into a neat, practical bob and she wore just a reluctant sliver of coral lipstick. The antithesis, in fact, of the look Emma had been trying to achieve!

* * *

'And Mr D'Amato would also prefer someone who speaks Japanese…' Evelyn continued.

'It didn't say that in the advertisement,' Emma pointed out. 'And you didn't mention it when we spoke on the telephone.'

'Luca—I mean Mr D'Amato—does not like to put too many specifications in the advertisements for one reason, and I rather agree…' she gave a small sniff '…that when the right person appears, we know.'

Well, there wasn't much Emma could say to that—clearly at first glance it had been decided that she wasn't the right person for the job.

Only…

Now, even though it had been an impossible dream, now that she *had* glimpsed it, Emma wanted it.

The salary was to die for—her family home, despite months on the market, hadn't sold and the nursing-home fees were piling up. Evelyn had explained during their initial telephone interview that Luca's staff burnt out quickly. He was a demanding boss, expecting complete devotion, and that this job and the travel would literally overtake her life, but that suited Emma just fine.

One year working hard and she could meet the nursing-home fees. Surely in that time the house would sell and pay off the backlog of debt? One year, burning herself out, and she would finally be free—free to pursue her dreams, free to live the life that had so far been denied her.

And now that glimmer of hope was rapidly being taken away. 'Now, if you'll excuse me…' Evelyn gave a thin attempt at a smile '…I have an important phone call to make.'

Well, at least Evelyn hadn't kept her guessing, at least she wouldn't be checking her phone every five minutes, or dashing to get the mail.

It couldn't have been made any clearer—she wasn't wanted.

'Well, thank you for seeing me…' She should just stand and go, shake Evelyn's hand and leave, except, inexplicably, she was dragging it out and for some stupid, stupid reason tears were threatening as yet another door closed on her push for a better future. 'Thank you for your time.'

It was her horoscope's fault, Emma told herself as Evelyn scribbled a note on her carefully prepared CV.

It had told her to *go for it*, reminded her that *you have to be in it to win it*. Told her that Jupiter and Mars had moved into her tenth house, which assured success in her career…

Stupid horoscopes, Emma thought as she went to retrieve her handbag. She didn't believe them anyway.

And then in he walked.

And the room went black.

Well, it didn't go black, but it might as well have, because *he* was all she could see.

Dressed in a tuxedo at four p.m., he strode over. Evelyn stood up, knotting his bow-tie as she gave him, in a couple of minutes, what seemed like a month's worth of messages, and all in a language that was foreign to Emma.

'Mr Hirosiko wants an "in person" next week.'

'No,' came his bored response.

'Kasumi was insistent.'

'He can have a face-to-face.

'And your sister rang, upset…she wants you there for the entire weekend.'

'Tell her that given that I'm paying for the entire weekend…' he had a thick, deep, Italian accent and Emma felt her toes curl '…I can choose my schedule.' His eyes drifted around the room as Evelyn dealt with his cufflinks and then he gave Emma a bored glance that changed midway and utter disinterest shifted slightly.

He deigned to give her a second look, and it was one she recognised well. It was the same look her father and brothers had used on unsuspecting women—at the petrol station, the supermarket, school concerts, the pub, oh, anywhere…

It was a look that to Emma screamed danger.

Six feet two with eyes of navy blue, Luca D'Amato might just as well have had the word *danger* stamped on his smooth forehead. Jet-black hair was slicked back, but a thick, raven lock escaped as Evelyn declared him officially knotted, and with one manicured hand he raked it back through his hair and it fell into effortless shape. Oh, she'd seen photos of him, had known that he was good-looking, but a grainy newspaper photo didn't do him justice, could never capture the essence of him, just the shocking presence of him. A scar ran the length of his left cheekbone, but that one imperfection merely enhanced his general faultlessness.

'We haven't been introduced.' Full, sensual lips curved into a smile as he turned come-to-bed eyes on her, his deep, accented voice for her ears now. 'This is…?'

Emma was struggling to find her voice, but Evelyn did it for her. 'Emma Stephenson.' Evelyn looked as if she were sucking lemons, and it dawned on Emma then that the *real* reason she hadn't got the job was perhaps that Evelyn had been hoping for someone plainer, dowdier, older, bigger…in fact, someone who would withstand Luca's charm. Well, she needn't have worried. Emma could handle Luca's sort with her hands tied behind her back—she'd grown up surrounded by them! 'We were just concluding the interview.'

'For the assistant PA job?' Luca checked, holding his hand out, and, because it was the polite thing to do, Emma shook it, feeling his warm fingers close around hers. Then she looked up as he voiced what she was thinking. 'But I've got a cold heart!' He winked at her.

'I'm sure you do!' Emma retorted. He was shameless, utterly shameless, and Evelyn was welcome to him. 'Well, again,' Emma said, coolly walking to the door, absolutely refusing to be rattled, 'thank you for your time.'

She walked out into the foyer, took the lift and only as she went to sign out did she realise that she'd forgotten her bag. That, despite appearances, despite appearing utterly and completely unruffled by his stunning presence, one glimpse of Luca D'Amato and her stomach was in knots. He was devastatingly handsome, with eyes that stripped, undressed and bedded you in a matter of seconds, and she had deliberately not returned the favour.

Emma headed back up in the elevator, moving to step out, only he was stepping in…

'I wasn't expecting to see you again.' He didn't move to let her pass him, his broad frame barring the exit, just slightly, and there was this offer of conversation that Emma didn't want to take up. 'I hear the interview didn't go too well.'

'It didn't.'

'Shame.'

How loaded with meaning was that single word, and Emma swallowed hard before speaking. 'I forgot my bag, I'm just going to get it,' she offered by way of explanation and as the lift door started to close she pressed the button to open it. There was this pang, this twinge, this snapping almost, this ending that she didn't want to happen, because he really was divine, and she wished for just a fleeting second that she had the looks, the confidence, the *experience* to allow him to pursue her.

But she didn't.

'Going down?' She pressed the 'hold' button for him, and he stood back as she stepped out and she caught the heavy scent of him, just the brush of his expensive suit as she passed by.

'No, up.' He grinned. 'To the roof.'

'Things that bad, then?' Emma called over her shoulder, safer now that the doors were closing, but he halted them with his hands.

'Do you want to join me?'

'I'm sure another job will come along,' she replied, watching a slow smile spread on his face as he got her dry humour. 'Things really are *never* that bad.'

'I'm actually going to Paris.'

'Lovely.'

'Helipad's on the roof.'

'They usually are.'

'Formal dinner, very boring, but maybe after… What are your plans?'

'TV dinner, a rerun of my favourite murder mystery.' Emma gave a sweet smile. 'So there's really no contest!'

He really was smiling now, thinking he'd got his easy way, holding the lift and waiting for her to step inside. So, *so* arrogant, so, *so* assuming, he really thought he could just snap his manicured fingers and summon her—he only seemed to get the message when she opened the doors to his office suite, his rich, assured voice just a touch perplexed.

'If you're worried that you've nothing to wear…'

'I'm not worried at all!' Emma laughed, and she could be as rude as she liked, could tell him exactly where to go with his smutty offer because, after all, he wasn't going to be her boss. 'As I said, there's really no contest!"

As the lift doors closed on him and she walked over to Evelyn's office, she was too irked to think before she knocked. Her hand rose, the door flung open and Emma stood there stunned as she took in the sight of Evelyn. The assured, pompous woman, who had dashed her hopes just a few moments before, was sobbing her heart out, first jumping up and shooing her out, appalled at being caught, then too upset to care.

'Negative!' she wept as Emma just stood there. 'I was so, so sure that I was.'

'I'm so sorry!' Well, what else could she say? 'I'm very sorry.'

And what could she do other than lead the sodden bundle to the nearest chair and peel off tissues as Evelyn gulped out her sorry tale?

Married five years.

Trying for a baby for four and a half of those.

IVF and injections and nasal sprays and tests and scans and egg retrieval.

And now she had to ring Paul and tell him, Evelyn had sobbed, had to ring her lovely, lovely husband, who wanted a baby as much as she did, and say that they'd failed to conceive through IVF for a second time.

Emma really didn't have to worry about saying the right thing, she couldn't get a word in. Instead, she just sat there and listened and poured water and offered tissues, and finally, when Evelyn had cried a river, she seemed to remember where she was and who she was talking to.

'You've been so nice—I mean, after I was so cool with you.'

'It's not a problem. If I'm not the right person...'

'No, you see...' Evelyn was wringing the tissue in her hands '...it has nothing to do with your experience or that you don't speak Japanese...'

'I know that now.'

'No, I mean—'

'I get it, okay? I admit, I assumed you must like him yourself, but...'

Emma giggled as Evelyn gave a watery smile and rolled her eyes. 'Not at all—I'm just sick of training new assistants, only to have them leave once he's bedded them. He's incorrigible, you know.'

'I know!' Emma groaned. 'He just asked me if I wanted to join him for dinner in Paris.' Emma smiled. 'Maybe you should look for a male PA.'

'They'd fall in love with him too,' Evelyn sighed, then she blinked. 'You said *no* to *Paris*?'

'Absolutely.'

'You don't find him attractive?' she gasped.

'He's divine,' Emma corrected her. 'He's side splittingly beautiful and any woman who says otherwise is a liar.'

'So why did you say no?' Evelyn wanted to know.

'Because I know him,' Emma explained. 'Not Luca personally, but I grew up amongst his type—I've read their rule book from cover to cover. I grew up in an all-male household—an exceptionally good-looking all-male household at that. '

'What about your mother?'

'She died when I was four.' Emma said, and there was nothing in her voice that requested sympathy—she merely stated the facts. 'My brothers are all considerably older than me...' She gave a thin smile at the memory of her childhood. 'And my father, well, a good-looking widower attracts a lot of admirers—all wanting to change him, all assuming he's just waiting for the next Mrs. Stephenson to come along—and he played them all well.'

'Luca's a nice man,' Evelyn said, just a touch pink at her own indiscretion in discussing her boss so personally. 'Beneath it all, when he's not being horrible, he's a really nice man. Take this assistant PA role that's currently being advertised—that's so I can cut back on my travel and late work nights...he's great really.'

'So long as you don't love him,' Emma said. 'So long as you have absolutely no intention or hope that one day you might change him...'

'You really *do* get it.' Evelyn blinked in wonder.

'I really do.' Locating her bag, Emma plonked it on her shoulder. 'I'd best get going.'

'And I'd better ring Paul.'

And it *had* been no contest—not for a second had she considered accepting Luca's extravagant offer, but sitting in her pyjamas, eating her TV dinner and watching the credits on her favourite show roll, the house was too big and too lonely for one.

Lonely...

She had never admitted it, not even to herself.

Oh, she had friends and a job and was kept busy—but sometimes, sometimes she wished she wasn't so wise, so cynical, so mistrusting where men were concerned.

She reached for a magazine, skipped straight to the problem page and read about other people's lives, other people's problems, and for the millionth time in her life she missed her mum. Missed the chats that would surely have happened about boys and men. Everyone else seemed to find it so easy—her friends fell in and out of love, skipped from relationship to relationship, and some were even getting married, or moving in with their boyfriends.

Yet Emma felt as if she'd been left at the starting post.

Too embarrassed by her brothers' teasing, too scared of getting hurt, she'd hid her first innocent crushes, had said no to dates in her teenage years, envying how others found this dating game so easy and just dived in and said yes.

Dear Barbara, she penned the letter in her head.

I'm an attractive twenty-four-year-old, I have friends, a job, a busy life and I'm still a virgin.

Oh, and I just said no to a night in Paris with the sexiest man on earth.

She'd make letter of the week!

And though it was great to have come home to no messages from her father's nursing home or new bills in the mail, all she felt was deflated. She flicked off the TV, and for just a second she faltered.

A tiny, wobbly second, where she wished she *were* stupid, wished for that impulse gene where men were concerned that had been so sorely denied her.

Wished she'd just said yes to Luca's dazzling offer.

Luca flicked through the channels on the television.

Not that he was watching it. It was on all day for background noise for the dog, Pepper—not that the animal appreciated it.

The night stretched on endlessly and he stood there, rueing the fact that he had been yawning and bored at eleven p.m. in Paris, but thanks to the time difference was wide awake and thoroughly restless at five minutes to midnight in London.

He should be exhausted, he had been up since five—but his head was clicking like an abacus. Hemming's, a large shopping chain, had called him in way too late to stop them from going under.

Except he *could* see a way to save them.

He grabbed a beer from the fridge and tried not to think about it, tried to wind down—just fed up with all the travel, with the demands. Why did everyone want an in-person—why couldn't they just settle for a face-to-face on a screen in the meeting room?

Hell, an email would usually suffice.

Sex would be nice.

And there were plenty who would be willing.

But he couldn't be bothered to talk.

Couldn't be bothered tonight to even pretend to be interested.

His tie must have been soldered on, along with his cufflinks—because he had to put down his drink to deal with them.

And deal with Pepper.

He snarled at the ginger miniature poodle, who snarled back at him. He let him out on his vast balcony to do whatever dogs did.

His maid would see to it in the morning.

Martha, an ex-girlfriend, had, after a trip back to his home in Sicily, decided to move in uninvited, and had conveniently forgotten Pepper when Luca had asked her to move out—three years ago!

'You,' Luca said, wandering back to the fridge and selecting a few choice morsels, 'are the most pathetic excuse for a dog I have ever seen.'

He ripped a chicken leg off and gnawed it as he stretched out on his sofa, with Pepper quivering on the floor beside him.

'You're on a diet.' Luca reminded him. Half watching a detective show on the television, finally Luca relented and threw some titbits to the floor in reward for their new game—having recently found out that if he changed the word 'Paw' to 'High five' the outcome was the same, only much more satisfying.

It had been hellish breaking up with Martha—her tears and protests at the unexpected end had been unprecedented—as over and over she had asked how he could end something so good.

And she'd left Pepper—just hadn't taken him, sure that Luca would crack and ring, would make contact—but what she hadn't truly realised was that when Luca ended things, he ended them.

That Luca would rather deal with a senile, smelly old dog than face her again.

The detective show actually wasn't that boring…

Three minutes from the end of the final episode of the season, Luca decided it was something he might actually get into.

And then the credits rolled.

And he knew this was what Emma had been talking about.

Knew she was watching it too.

He just knew it. And he wished she'd said yes to Paris.

CHAPTER TWO

IT WAS a quarter to five on a Thursday afternoon and the entire staff of D'Amato Financiers, excluding Emma, seemed to be abuzz with excitement. As Emma walked back from a meeting with the manager of HR she could see make-up, slyly in some cases and blatantly in others, being applied at desks, and the general office area reeked of a clash of newly sprayed perfume. Even the guys were at it—appearing from the men's room with a generous dash of newly applied hair product and a glint in their eyes as the end of the workday approached.

Thursday night in London, and it seemed everyone had plans.

Everyone except Emma.

She remembered with a pang when Thursday nights had heralded the start of the weekend. When Friday morning had been spent huddled around the coffee machine, dissecting the previous night.

She'd be lucky if she was out of here by seven *and* she had to visit her father *and* she had to be back here by six the next morning, to meet with Luca and then fly up for an eight-thirty a.m. meeting in Scotland.

Evelyn had had second thoughts—offering Emma the position the following day—and she had been in her dream job for six weeks now. And though it was still just that, a dream job, it was also extremely hard work—as Assistant Personal Assistant to Luca D'Amato, it wasn't just her job title that took some explaining. Every minute of Luca's time was valuable, Evelyn had explained on her first day. Beyond valuable, actually— which was why he had his own travel team, two assistants and looking for a third, four full-time drivers, in fact a whole fleet of staff that took care of the details and allowed Luca to get on with doing what he did best—rescuing struggling companies, turning them around and making an obscene amount of money in the process.

Emma's job was varied, mostly exciting and yet also downright boring at times—dealing with his sister's wedding, his dog, his housekeeper's endless reams of days off. The list was endless.

Ducking into the ladies' room, Emma knew she ought to attempt a quick repair job on her hair and face before she headed back to her office and to whatever mood Luca was in, but it took for ever to elbow her way to the mirror and her curly dark hair had spent too long in an air-conditioned building because it was looking decidedly frizzy. She borrowed a squirt of serum from a snooty-looking redhead, re-tied her hair back in a low ponytail and then, sick of the coffee on the top floor, she grabbed a hot chocolate and a bag of crisps from the vending machine then headed back up in the lift, knowing that in all likelihood this would double up as dinner.

'Louse!'

As she walked out of the lift, Emma stepped back as a stunning, raven-haired woman stormed out of Luca's office and into the lift, tears streaming down her face but watching his closed office door and just standing there, waiting for it to open, waiting for him to follow her out, to call her back, to no doubt tell her that it didn't have to end like this, that he'd had a change of heart.

Of course he didn't.

Of course he wouldn't—no one delivered an ultimatum to Luca and came out smiling, not even this rare beauty, who, with a sob of frustration, finally pushed the lift button, her desperate eyes peeking out of the closing gap, still hoping that Luca would change his mind.

'That,' he said, first peering around the door and making sure it was safe to come out, 'was not my fault.' He put up his hands in bemusement and said it again. 'Really, that time it wasn't my fault.' Still Emma said nothing, just watched with pursed lips as he helped himself to her hot chocolate, as he always did if she didn't pour it into her mug before he saw it. 'Honestly, it wasn't!'

'It never is.' Sarcasm dripped from Emma's lips, which might seem rude to some, and might be no way to talk to your boss—but it was because she did speak to him like that, because she did keep him at arm's length and because she was very good at her job, that, despite his stunning initial offer, in the six weeks she had worked there, Luca hadn't even attempted to flirt.

Well, the odd time perhaps!

But it was quickly, expertly, rebuffed.

'Did you get my messages?' Emma checked, because he never read them. 'A Dr Calista called—he wants you to ring him.'

'Fine.'

'And your sister too—she wants to know if you've looked at the ties.'

'Ties?'

'She sent you an email of some photos of ties— for the groomsmen to wear at the wedding—and she wants to know if you're staying. She's rung a few times today.'

'Remind her of my hourly rate,' Luca drawled, 'and if she keeps ringing, bill her.'

He didn't mean it, Emma knew that, but he could be so scathing at times.

'I *do* mean it,' Luca said as if in response to her private thoughts.

'You really want me to bill your sister for ringing you?' She *knew* he didn't mean it, knew he'd hit the roof if she actually did it, and just refused to play his games.

'I want you,' Luca said, very firmly, very clearly, 'to practise some of the assertion this job demands—I am not to be bothered with these details, is that clear?'

'Very.'

'Good.' Luca said. '*You* choose the ties, *you* sort things out and you have my full authority to tell her it was me.'

'Fine.'

He was turning now, heading back to his office,

tossing the empty chocolate cup in the bin. Then he turned around.

'Are you doing anything tonight?'

'Actually, yes,' Emma said through gritted teeth, 'I've got plans.'

'Well, cancel them.' Luca shrugged. 'Ruby was supposed to be coming with me to some awful dinner dance at Hemming's. It's plus one, so I'm expected to bring someone.'

'I really *do* have plans!' Emma repeated, because she was beginning to get tired of this— she worked hard, more than hard, but this would be the fourth night in a row that she hadn't got to visit her father and it simply wasn't fair— surely she was allowed to have a semblance of a life? 'I need to visit my father,' she reluctantly explained, loath to let Luca in on her personal life. 'I told him I'd be over tonight.'

'So, tell him that you are working.'

'I've been putting him off all week.' She just couldn't do it to him *again*. 'I'd really like to finish on time tonight.' When Luca just frowned, she pushed a touch further. 'Look, I don't usually say no, but surely there's someone else you can ask?'

Which was a stupid thing to say. There were plenty of women Luca could ask, and there was one reason and one reason only that he was asking her! 'I was hoping for an early night,' Luca sighed. 'At least with you it would be just dinner!' Which was a rather strange compliment, but it bought a reluctant smile to her face. 'I'll ask Evelyn—where is she, by the way?'

'No, don't...' Emma flustered, for Evelyn had sneaked off to the doctor's to pick up her vials and needles for her final round of IVF, which she was starting in the morning. The last thing the poor woman needed was a night on the town with Luca. 'I'll just go. It's fine.'

'You're sure?' Luca frowned, just a touch guilty now that he had got his own way, as he knew full well where Evelyn was. 'Tell you what—we can visit your father on the way.'

'We can't,' Emma fretted. 'I'll be in evening dress!'

'So?' Luca grinned. 'Go on, get ready and we'll leave in an hour.'

It was testament to the nature of her job that she *could* get ready for a formal function within the hour. There was a bathroom on their floor and Emma stuffed her curls under a cap and quickly showered. She even had a wardrobe in her office—her day bag was already packed and ready for her jaunt to Scotland in the morning and Emma rummaged in it for her styling wand and spare make-up bag then set to work on her face, squirting drops in her eyes in the hope they'd sparkle and then working on her lips and cheeks.

With some difficulty she pulled stockings onto damp legs and then slipped on her fast-becoming-familiar little black dress and clipped on a string of black pearls, before coaxing tired feet into stilettos.

And then she tackled her hair. Spritzing her

wayward, corkscrew curls around the wand and trying to coax them into shape.

It was a routine she was starting to perfect.

'You need some more evening wear,' was Luca's only comment when he saw that she was in her black dress again.

'Just as soon as I get a day off!' Emma retorted. 'Aren't you ready?'

He didn't answer but, then, Luca rarely answered pointless questions. Instead, he strode out to the lifts with Emma following behind, holding a small suitcase to take to her father and stuffing her evening bag with keys and lipstick and hair serum and sticking plasters as the lift plummeted down.

'I forgot to put on perfume.'

He sniffed the air. 'You smell fine.'

Men!

He glanced at the small case she was carrying, but didn't comment and neither did Emma, not bothering with small talk. She just sat in the back of the car with Luca as they moved at a snail's pace through the heavy peak-hour traffic, a knot of tension in her stomach, sure that at any moment he'd tell her it was too late to stop by her father's nursing home. Glancing at her watch, she realised they weren't going to be able to make it and it was actually a relief—she didn't want to explain her life to Luca.

'The old dog's home first!" Luca drawled, not knowing the nerve he was pricking as he let them into his apartment. The television was blaring as usual and Emma paced as Luca chopped up some chicken breast and added a spoonful of rice to Pepper's bowl.

'He's on a diet,' Luca explained.

She didn't quite get where Pepper fitted into the scheme of things. She'd been to Luca's apartment on several occasions and still couldn't work out what Luca was doing with a dog. Neither man nor beast seemed to particularly like each other and the last thing a person with Luca's schedule needed was a dog—and a lapdog at that.

But it wasn't her place to question. It was her

job to just book the vet in for home visits, or make sure that the dog sitter knew when Luca was suddenly called away.

'Look in the bathroom,' Luca called from the bedroom. 'There is probably some perfume there that has been left behind—help yourself.'

It was like the beauty section in a chemist's shop—perfumes, lipsticks, body lotions, all left behind by their previous owners—but it wasn't them that caught her attention. In the mirror she could see Luca's reflection—dressed in black hipster underwear, he was selecting an evening shirt, and though she was getting used to Luca, she wasn't used to seeing quite so much of him.

He was stunning.

He was so pompous and arrogant that for the most part Emma was able to switch off from the fact he was, quite simply, the most beautiful man she had ever seen—only now she was *seeing* him.

He had long muscular legs that even managed to look sexy in socks. As he pulled on his shirt, she caught more than a glimpse of his chest, a smattering of black hair that made Emma's toes curl in her already too tight shoes. Dragging her eyes away, she selected some perfume and squirted it on, but her eyes wandered back to the stunning view of him, to those long lean legs as he sat on the bed and pulled on his trousers.

And then he caught her looking.

His eyes held hers in the mirror for an indecently long time, a ghost of a smile spreading on his lips, and then she snapped her eyes away.

'Ready?' So flustered was Emma that his voice in the doorway made her jump. 'If we want to stop at your father's, we'd better leave.'

He knew.

Cheeks burning, her back and thighs pressed into the leather seat of Luca's car, Emma knew that he knew.

That despite the banter, despite the rebuffs, despite her thoroughly cool demeanour around him—Luca D'Amato knew that he moved her.

And suddenly, for the first time in six weeks, Emma felt vulnerable.

CHAPTER THREE

'SO WHERE does he live?'

Emma gave the driver the address and sat back in her seat, her tension mounting as the car neared the leafy street, lined with huge impressive homes.

'It's nice here...' Luca glanced out of the window. 'So, is this where you grew up?'

He had no idea, must just assume that her father could afford a house in this area, but instead of answering she just shook her head, tempted to tell the driver to forget it and take them straight to the Hemmings' dinner dance, except her father would be devastated if she rang and cancelled again.

'After that red car on the left...' Emma instructed the driver. 'Just here will do.' Only he went past the red car and pulled up at the gates, pressing the button in the intercom. Emma could feel her cheeks burning as Luca took in the nursing home sign. 'Could you tell them Mr Stephenson's daughter is here for a visit?'

'I'll wait in the car.' She could feel Luca's eyes on her as he spoke, but couldn't look at him, just climbed out as the driver handed her the small suitcase.

'I shouldn't be long.'

'Hi, Dad!'

The way his face lit up when she walked into his room only made her feel worse. He looked forward so much to her visits, but lately they had been becoming fewer and further between.

'You look like your mum...' Frank beamed '...when we used to go out dancing.' And on and on he chatted as Emma put away his laundered pyjamas and replaced his deodorant and talc and filled up his little dish with money for a newspaper in the morning. And it seemed like a nice visit because her father was chatty and for once there wasn't a hint of malice about her mother, but it hurt more than she could explain.

His face had never used to light up when Emma had walked in the room—that had only started to happen in these past few months. Growing up, he'd practically ignored her, or when he did talk to her, it was to bad-mouth her mother, as if it had been her fault she'd died. So in all it had been a pretty wretched excuse of a childhood and Emma knew she had every reason to walk away, to leave it to the system to look after him. Only now, since his stroke, it was as if her horrible childhood had somehow been erased. For the first time they had a father-daughter relationship, for the first time she was hearing little bits about her mother, about her history, and despite it all, he was her dad—and even if they'd left it rather late they did have a relationship and she could never, like her brothers had, bring herself to just walk away from him.

'I'm sorry I haven't been in more recently.' She broke his favourite chocolate she had brought him into pieces and put some on a plate in front of him. 'Work's so busy…but I'll be in properly at the weekend.'

'You have to go?' Frank's eyes filled with tears. 'You've only just got here.'

'Dad, I have to work.'

She felt awful leaving him so soon—except she had no choice. Until the house sold, it was her work that was paying for the home.

She knew what the nurses must think of her as she clipped past the desk in high heels, and she was so close to crying it hurt—she was tired, so tired of juggling things, of scrambling to get everything half done. At work she was calm and efficient, yet on the inside she was a festering mess.

'Miss Stephenson.' As the cool night air hit her she gulped it in, turning to see who was following her. Aware Luca must be watching, she died inside as the supervisor waved an all too familiar manila envelope. 'We've been trying to contact you about the account.'

'I spoke with Accounts yesterday...' Emma tried to keep her voice even, tried to lower her shoulders and pretend, for Luca if he was watching, that there was nothing wrong. 'I explained that I have a new job, that I'm catching up on the outstanding balance—they're putting a new payment plan in place.'

'I'm aware of that—it's here for you in writing.'

She took the envelope. 'Thank you.'

'Any default on this plan and I'm afraid...'

'There won't be.' Emma swallowed. 'You know Dad's house is on the market.'

'We have a long waiting list,' the supervisor answered. 'We're trying to help, Miss Stephenson, but we're not a charity.'

The car was full of music when she entered, and Luca was sending emails on his phone. She breathed out a sigh of relief that he surely hadn't noticed the uncomfortable exchange with the supervisor.

'How was he?' Luca checked.

'A bit teary,' Emma admitted. 'Still, I'll see him properly at the weekend.'

'Does he get other visitors...?' His voice trailed off. Evelyn had told him about her mother's death and, seeing Emma's tight lips, he changed tack. 'It looks like a nice place,' Luca commented, glancing up at the impressive building as the car crunched out of the driveway. 'Expensive?'

'A bit.' Emma shrugged. 'You do what you can.'

Unexpectedly, Emma found herself enjoying the Hemmings' dinner dance.

It wasn't an exceptionally lavish function they attended—that was the type of thing that had got the company into a mess in the first place—but it was a genuine, feel-good party and Luca was the man everyone wanted to greet. His prowess had salvaged a sinking ship and in the process had saved hundreds of jobs.

And Luca was a very nice date.

He turned off his phone the moment they arrived and he remembered to introduce her to enough people so that when he was circulating she didn't feel like a complete spare part. He even swapped his white chocolate and nougat mousse with her when she got landed with the almond torte, and when the dancing started he didn't ditch her just because she was a work date, even though on many occasions he could have. In fact, apart from one duty dance with the CEO's wife and a long conversation with some potential investors, Luca for once appeared off duty.

'Thank you…' He held her loosely in his arms as they danced. 'I know you had other things to do tonight.'

'It's actually been nice.'

'It has,' Luca agreed. 'I was worried, I admit.'

'I'm sure you'd have found someone else to join you.'

'I meant, I was worried whether I could salvage them from bankruptcy,' he explained, and he laughed at her blush. 'I do think about work sometimes.'

'Sometimes!' Emma laughed. 'I don't know how you fit it all in.'

'I just do.' He stared down at her. 'And so do you.' He looked down at her for a long moment. 'How long has he been there?' All evening he had made no comment about her father, yet the question had hung between them.

'Six months.'

'You are very young for him to be…'

'Dad was quite a bit older than Mum.'

'Oh.'

'He had a stroke at the beginning of the year…' Her voice trailed off, she didn't want to talk about it, she really, really didn't. Yes, tonight was work, but in his arms, swaying to the music, when Luca didn't push or press the point, really it was just a relief to be here, to be away from it all, even for just a little while.

'I am glad it is you tonight,' Luca said. And close to midnight, with champagne inside her, it would have been very easy to lean closer, very, worryingly easy to rest her head on that chest that was just inches from her, terribly, terribly easy to wonder at his words. So to stop herself, she reminded herself of the real reason that she was here, and couldn't help herself from asking.

'What happened with Ruby?' She spoke to his lips, the same way that he was speaking to hers, and suddenly it wasn't working. Reminding herself of his appalling reputation wasn't keeping her safe—she was having to forcibly resist the urge to move closer to him.

'She said those four little words.'

'Three little words!' Emma corrected, because occasionally his excellent English slipped.

'No, four...' She could see the shadow of growth on his chin, his full mouth moving as he spoke, feel his breath and wished suddenly he'd just kiss her. 'Where is this leading?'

She could only smile at her own stupidity as realisation hit, and was so, so glad she hadn't quickly answered what she had briefly assumed was a question, because it took a second to work out he wasn't talking about them—he was answering her question about Ruby.

'So I told her—nowhere!

'Come on,' he said as the music ended and he broke away, 'let's go. I'm staying at the office. We have a helicopter to catch…' he squinted at his watch '…in five hours.' Which translated to about three hours' sleep if she went home. 'What about you?

That extra hour actually counted when you were operating on Luca time.

Ever the gentleman, he pulled out the sofa bed in her office then retired to his luxury suite. Emma lay staring at the ceiling, thinking about him. Not once had he pounced on her, had never made her feel uncomfortable, and apart from that blistering first invitation, there had been nothing else.

Except he'd caught her looking at him earlier.

Emma squirmed in embarrassment and then

consoled herself that if she'd been standing in her bra and panties, he'd have had a quick peek too.

It offered no consolation.

'What's the point of it all, Em?'

His voice over the intercom penetrated the darkness and made her smile. He did this every now and then.

'So you can make pots of money,' she responded.

'I've made pots of money.'

'So you can have any woman you want.'

There was a pensive pause.

'I have any woman I want.'

'I don't know, then.'

'So why are you here?' Luca asked. 'Working yourself into the ground, that cruel boss never giving you a night off?'

'Because I love my work!' she duly answered.

'Rubbish!' came the voice over the intercom, and Emma smiled. 'Why *are* you here Em?'

She paused for the longest time—almost expecting the door to open and Luca to walk in. This conversation, despite taking place over an intercom, was surprisingly intimate. And lying in dark, she was almost tempted to tell him, about the bills and the house, about her dream of going to art school. About how this job was her lifeline, about how, one day, she hoped it might set her up to pursue her goals…

Which was hardly the conversation to have with your boss.

''Night, Luca!'

She could never have guessed but save for those two words her office door would have opened.

He liked her.

Luca stared up at the familiar ceiling, at the dimmed lights that never actually went off—and it was a measure of how much he liked her that he didn't go to her.

It had nothing to do with Evelyn's stern warnings—well, maybe a bit, as Evelyn was too good to lose, and her husband was getting less and less impressed with the hours his wife put in.

But it was more than that.

He didn't want to lose Emma.

He liked her.

Not just liked her, but actually *liked* her.

Liked having her in his day.

She was nothing like anyone he'd met before. She brightened up the office with her chatter and her fizz and she answered him back and made him smile.

And she liked him too. In *that* way.

He'd actually been beginning to wonder—he'd been a bit taken aback when she'd so coolly turned him down at their first meeting. Working with him, she was so on guard, so scathing of his ways, that he'd wondered if the reason he liked her was that she was the one woman who didn't fancy him.

Then tonight he'd seen her expression in the mirror, and in that second before she'd realised he'd caught her, he had seen the want in her eyes.

He lay racked with rare indecision.

His instinct was to let nature take its course.

With women, Luca always followed instinct—and instinct told him to go out there to where she lay, in those ugly pyjamas she wore. Luca became instantly hard at the thought of those curls on the pillow, and her soft skin.

So why the reticence?

Because it would last a couple of weeks, a couple of months perhaps—and then she'd want more from him, like they all did, like Martha had…

He closed his eyes on that sudden thought, but circles of light still danced before his eyes.

Martha had been the only one it had *really* hurt to let go.

It was a thought that till now had comforted him—that he had said goodbye to *the one*, that the hardest part of the deal he had made all those years ago was over.

So why, when he hadn't so much as kissed Emma, was he comparing her to Martha?

He hadn't seen anyone since Emma had joined the staff, had finally dumped Ruby, whom he'd kept dangling for weeks.

He thought about going out there to Emma— *how* he thought about going out there—but something stopped him: she really needed this job and for now, at least, he wanted her around.

He couldn't have both.

CHAPTER FOUR

'YOUR sister is insisting that she speak with you. She's tried your mobile, she's been calling all morning,' Emma said to the silence of the intercom. 'And now she is insisting.'

'I'm still in a meeting.'

Luca did everything the other way around from anyone else she had met: he didn't drop a thing for family! He had several mobile phone numbers—yet his family all went directly to message bank, no exception, no deviation. Emma knew he checked them—had seen him listen, scowl and hit 'delete', yet unless *he* was in the right frame of mind, Luca refused to pick up.

Which left Emma to deal with the fallout.

'I'm sorry, Daniela,' she said for the umpteenth

time. 'He really can't be disturbed—is there anything that I can help you with?'

'You can ask why he no come, why all he can give me on my special day is two hours of his precious time, familia *is everything, my own brother…'* It really was rather draining to listen to, yet she was being paid fabulously to do so. And dealing with Daniela's histrionics was actually easier than dealing with Luca right now—as the wedding approached his mood blackened. Oh, nothing had been said, he was still his fastidious, energetic self, barking orders, making her laugh every now and then, but there was this tension to him that was palpable—this grey, gathering cloud that seemed to be following him wherever he went.

'I'm going over to Hemming's.' Evelyn came to her desk. 'Luca needs some files and I have to speak with the accountant.'

'Sure.'

'Whatever you do, Emma—' Evelyn's voice was serious '—don't put Daniela through—with

Luca in this mood, he'll surely say something he regrets and guess who will have to deal with it?'

'What is going on?' Emma asked for the fiftieth time. 'Why can't he just go for the weekend? He does it for his clients all the time.'

'I've no idea.' Suddenly Emma realised Evelyn wasn't putting her off with vague answers. 'I've worked for Luca for years now and have had little to do with his family, but since this wedding was announced, they're on the phone every five minutes, and it's doing nothing to improve his mood.'

'I had worked that one out.'

'Get me Dr Calista on the phone.' Luca's voice through the intercom was a brusque order and Evelyn rolled her eyes as Emma picked up the phone.

'Good luck.'

It was rather like knowing there was a wild bear in the building with the door unlocked.

Luca wandered out every now and then, snarling and sniping, giving his orders and then retreating. The phones were ringing red hot and with Evelyn out, Emma rang the deli and had some sandwiches sent up for her own lunch. Luca had snapped, when she'd asked him, that he didn't want anything.

'What's in them?' He peered at her lunch and selected the smoked salmon and cream cheese without a word, but Emma was used to him now, and the second he slammed the door of his office she opened her drawer and pulled out her *own* smoked salmon and cream cheese sandwiches, smiling at her own foresight as she picked up the phone.

She wasn't smiling now—the sandwich like sawdust in her mouth as she faced a new challenge, wondering if she should ring Evelyn and check, completely unsure what to do.

'Luca...' she swallowed the mouthful of water she had quickly taken '...it's your mother on the phone.'

'I'll call her later,' came the curt reply.

Which she relayed, to no avail.

'Luca…' She felt as if she were pressing the demolition button as she pressed the intercom again.

'What?'

'She's crying. I don't know if something's happened…'

When he swore in Italian, Emma held her breath, hardly letting it out when she saw the red light on and realised he had taken the call, wondering if she had done the right thing. The thick door to his office meant she could hear nothing and Emma paced up and down, staring at the red light, knowing they were talking, wondering if she should go in and apologise afterwards, berating herself for not checking with Evelyn what she should do in these circumstances. And then, after an interminable time, the red light went off.

She waited a moment for his angry summons but, worse than that, there was only silence and a closed door.

She knocked—as he insisted she did.

And knocked again, ignoring that he didn't

answer—deciding to 'practise some of the assertion this job demands'. Taking a deep breath, she walked in. Afterwards, she fervently wished she hadn't, but by then it was already too late.

He couldn't stand it—he just couldn't *stand* it!

For weeks Daniela had been ringing, every day, then every hour, and now and then his mother too.

And now had come the tears.

The pleading.

'*Familia, Luca.*'

He hated *familia*!

'Just this—all I ask of you, all I have done for you, all I have *suffered* for you!'

For him?

Always his mother twisted things—and she was twisting them now, telling him she had suffered for him, that she had taken the beatings, the hell, the agony—*for* him.

And now, supposedly, he had to repay the favour.

He *hated* this!

There was a rip of anger in him, this fury that sixteen years living away from home had only slightly dimmed, because it was always there, churning beneath the surface. His vast office was tiny, too small to contain his fury, his loathing, his hate.

Then he became distantly aware that his mobile was ringing.

Ma.

Ma.

Ma.

He picked the mobile up and threw it across the room—but still it rang.

He picked up his landline phone and tossed that too.

Ah, but soon would come the emails…

So with one swoop he cleared his entire desk of its contents, the computer, papers, his lamp, his coffee, everything, crashing in one swoop, a smash of glass and chaos, with no relief, no reprieve because Emma walked in.

'Out!'

He roared it at her, but she just stood there, frozen.

'*Get out now!*' Except she didn't, just stood there eyes wide in shock and then, worse, with tears in them...refusing to leave, refusing to go. So he stormed out of his office and on to the lift, pounded on the button and then gave in, resting his head on his forearm and dragging in air.

He would explain.

He must explain.

He hadn't wanted her to see him like that...

Luca turned and walked back, calmer now, together now, and then he saw her.

Kneeling on the floor, crying and scared and shaking, picking up the lamp, retrieving shards of glass—trying to clear up the chaos so that it might appear to have never happened.

It could have been his mother twenty years ago—only this time it was *he* who had caused the chaos, and *he* who had reduced Emma to frightened tears.

'I'm sorry!' Her voice was shaky as she took

the blame, and that was what almost killed Luca. 'I should never have put her through to you.'

It almost killed him, because Luca realised with a dread that had been building for years now—he *was* turning into his father.

CHAPTER FIVE

EMMA had grown up with men long enough to refuse to tiptoe around them—oh, she steered clear of Luca for a while and when Evelyn came back a new lamp was purchased, a few items replaced, and supposedly it had never happened.

Except it had.

Yet she refused to be silenced.

Refused to dance around him and refused not to question him when a ridiculous plan made itself known.

'Can you tell me why *I'm* booked to attend your sister's wedding?' Emma struggled to keep her voice even—after all, this was her boss and this *had* to be a mistake, but she wasn't going to take *this*!

It was six p.m. and Emma had spent the last two hours with Luca's travel team, working out the logistics of his impossible schedule for the upcoming fortnight, only to see her name appear on the flight list for Palermo and the transfer helicopter to his village. Worse than that, she'd had to suffer the thinly veiled smirk on the travel team manager's face when she'd asked why the hotel hadn't yet been booked.

There were no hotels in the village!

'Oh!' Luca had at least the grace to wince. 'I've been meaning to tell you…' Luca could read women as easily as a newspaper and as her eyes widened at his choice of words, he quickly corrected himself. 'I mean, *ask* you.'

'Ask me what?' she asked through gritted teeth.

'You know my sister is getting married soon.'

'Is she really?' Emma feigned surprise. After all, *she* was the one co-ordinating the lavish wedding gift—a pool, and not just any pool, an infinity pool cut into the edge of the volcanic rock no less. And *she* was the one who had been dealing with the Sicilian foreman and the architect and the insurance company, the tie selection people, the sister and the mother, not to mention Luca's appalling mood! Oh, yes, she knew his sister was getting married!

'Please,' Luca said. 'Sarcasm doesn't suit you.' He frowned for a moment, then added, 'Actually, it does—but not now. I need some help over the weekend. It's a bit hard to explain...'

She gave a tiny shake of her head. Luca *never* found things hard to explain—the Luca she knew always just came out and said what he meant.

'Well, I can't help. I actually have plans that weekend,' Emma said, her voice still even and calm. She didn't actually—even though it was her birthday, she'd made no plans other than visiting her father, but she certainly wasn't going to let Luca know that. 'And I know my job is varied, but playing the part of wedding planner is really out of my league.'

'The wedding is all taken care of.'

'So what do you need me for?'

'It would make things easier, to have someone there with me,' he admitted.

'You mean *with* you?' She was really shaking her head now. 'No, Luca, absolutely not. You could ask anyone…'

'But you're not going to go and get any stupid ideas,' Luca said. 'Emma, you understand me. The last woman I brought home…' He gave a small swallow before he named her. 'Martha. I explained to her not to get swept away, that my family would assume we were serious, that they would think that there was a wedding imminent. She assured me she understood, except when we got there…'

'Things changed?'

Luca nodded. 'I can't face going; I can't stand the thought of being in the same house for two, maybe three nights on my own.' He looked at her then, at her dark curls bobbing, at the mouth that could always somehow make him laugh, at the body he thought of at night now. *This* was the one way he could do it—with the one woman who could make hell bearable right now beside him.

Even if it meant he would soon have to say goodbye to her…

'I thought that with you there…'

'Did you really think I'd say yes?' Emma demanded. 'Well, obviously you did if the travel team already know about it.'

'I was going to speak to you later this afternoon. I didn't realise the meeting had been brought forward.'

'Well, the answer would have been the same—no!'

'You're making this a bigger deal than it is!' he protested.

'It's a very big deal to *me*! Anyway, there are any number of women who would be more than happy to accommodate you. Ask one of them.'

'My father's ill!' He played the sympathy card, but Emma just gave him a wide-eyed look.

'So is mine—but I'm not asking you to share a bed with me,' she retorted.

'He has just a couple of months to live,' Luca revealed.

'I'm sorry to hear that,' Emma responded, 'but I can't help. Look…' she was irritated now. More than irritated, she was angry at his assumption that he could just go ahead and organise something like this without even consulting her. 'I'm sorry he's ill, but—'

'I'm not sorry he's ill, Emma,' he interrupted her, his voice dark. 'I hate my father—really, the end cannot come soon enough. My mother has asked, pleaded that I come, that for one final time we put on the D'Amato show…'

'The D'Amato show?' Emma frowned, but Luca didn't elaborate.

'I cannot face it.' She'd never heard him anything other than assured and the plea for understanding in his voice momentarily swayed her. 'I'm asking you because I know you get it…'

'Get *what*?'

'Me!' For the first time he looked uncomfortable. 'I have no interest in marriage, no interest in settling down—not ever. You understand…'

he gave an irritated shrug '…that this would be strictly business.'

'Sharing your bed isn't *my* idea of business!'

'You'd be well remunerated…' He took in her furious expression and hastily added, 'We could just say you're my girlfriend—I'm not asking for sex!'

'Just as well, because I absolutely do not fancy you!' Emma turned to go, her face burning. She'd heard enough, lied enough but she hadn't actually said enough. She turned back. 'You're right, Luca—I do *get* you. And, yes, I get your good looks and your sentiments where women are concerned. I get that you have no desire to settle down and that women want more—I get it all. Well, enough to know that you rarely sleep alone, and no matter how you introduce me to your family or what you think may or may not happen between us while we're away, but you and I, sharing a bed, well, it wouldn't work!'

'I think it would work rather well!' he retaliated.

And just then there was a tiny shift, a brief

moment when they were both imagining it, both thinking about it, both visiting the same place for a very dangerous second. She suddenly felt hot and bothered—partly, to be honest, because he simply oozed sexuality—and yet it wasn't actually just about him and whether or not he deigned to lay a finger on her, whether or not he could keep to the spirit of any agreement they might come to.

It was also about the fact that she was twenty-four and had never had a relationship—sometimes she felt as if she was the last virgin around! Oh, she had made the excuse that she had been too busy looking after her father and in part that was true—but it was about more than that. She was far too guarded with her heart, far too mistrusting of men, and with Luca that was wise.

Except…

With Luca, at least she'd know where she stood from the very start.

He watched the small swallow in her throat, watched her cheeks dust pink.

And then she thought of his reaction when he found out she was a virgin—which snapped her mind away from the very dangerous place it had been dwelling.

'The answer's still no.' Very firmly she said it.

'Can I ask you to at least think about it?' he pressed.

'I already have and I've given my answer. I like working for you, Luca.' She bared her teeth in a standoffish smile. 'Let's just keep things professional, shall we? If you're able to!' And with that, she walked out.

Which told him.

For the first time Luca was the one blushing—not that anyone would notice, but he could feel his ears burn just a touch as she dismissed him, put him in his place. Just as she always did, Luca realised as he sat, smarting, at his desk. Unused to rejection, it didn't sit well with him at all.

He could have anyone he wanted! With that thought, he pulled out his phone and scrolled through the list of contacts, looking at the names of the many beauties around the globe he could summon right now, this very minute—only recently none had really appealed.

Emma did.

He sat there for ages, thinking, going over and over it in his mind, as the office darkened.

Emma could get him through these next few weeks—the wedding, the last stages of his father's illness. *How* much more bearable it would be with Emma around… And why did it only have to be for just a few weeks? He had no qualms that they would get on—despite her protests, he knew she was attracted to him.

So why would it have to end so soon? Maybe it could be a few months, or even as much as a year…

He went to turn on the desk lamp, but though Evelyn had managed a close replica, the cord was on the other side, and in that second, as he reached for thin air, Luca was reminded why a relationship with Emma could never last even as long as that.

He pulled up a document on screen.

Position Vacant
Assistant PA

He read the guidelines and then added a few more words.

'Fluent Japanese essential.'

Save the changes?

Emma knocked and he called her in. 'I just need a file, if that's okay…'

'Sure.'

'I brought you coffee.' She didn't appear in the least uncomfortable when she came in and placed his strong brew on his desk. In her own way, Luca realised, she was setting the tone, heading over to the filing cabinet and carrying on efficiently, as if their previous conversation had never happened.

She was absolutely gorgeous, Luca mused. Her hair was working its way out of its low ponytail, dark curls dancing around her face, and he sat watching her thin jumper strain over her generous breasts as she pulled over the foot ladder and still had to stretch to reach the top file.

She had a fantastic bottom.

Round and curvy and soft.

What *was* this fascination with Emma?

She was nothing like the women he usually dated—he usually liked his women trim and groomed to within an inch of their lives and preferably without an opinion.

Emma had an opinion on everything.

'Go home,' he said, irritated with himself now. He just wanted the temptation of her out of there.

'Oh!' She glanced at her watch. 'Are you sure?'

'It's your art class tonight, isn't it?'

She'd missed the last two weeks, and Emma was touched that he'd noticed. 'Is there anything else you need before I go?'

He chose not to answer that one.

He'd get to that soon enough.

CHAPTER SIX

'EMMA!'

There were many ways Luca said her name, and with his rich Italian accent the first couple of thousand times he had made her rather plain name sound vaguely exotic.

Just not any more.

This was a short brusque *'Emma'* that came over her intercom and jolted her out of the notes she was compiling, a clipped order that he wanted her to come into his office now.

She had a nine a.m. meeting with HR that she *had* to be at in a five minutes—a meeting about which he would want a full written report on his desk by lunchtime, with question time after, no doubt. She was tempted to ignore his summons, let him think that she had already left.

'Emma!' The voice was just as curt, only this time it came not from the intercom but from the man himself—clearly she hadn't responded within the requisite two seconds.

'Didn't you hear me?'

'I was just coming,' Emma said calmly.

It had been a week since Luca had put forward his ridiculous proposition—and though he'd had the good sense not to broach it again, the mood between them wasn't great.

He wasn't sulking exactly but, as Emma had demanded, things were strictly businesslike and the chatter and banter had gone—and she missed it. Working such ridiculous hours, he consumed a large part of her day, and she missed that side of him, that was all.

'I need you to set up a meeting with Mr Hirosiko. I need all the latest figures…'

Luca had recently set his giddy sights on Japan—a difficult market to break into for an outsider, only Luca had seen it as a challenge, zipping through a refresher course of the language, instructing Emma and Evelyn to learn it too, and when Luca focused, he really focused. Not only did he brush up on etiquette skills but he was suddenly into *kaiseki ryori*, or Japanese haute cuisine, his restless mind constantly seeking challenges, new interests. He never tired; instead, he just absorbed the new energy and expanded, moving on to the next challenge while retaining the old.

'Set up the meeting room for a face-to-face.' He snapped his fingers as he tried to recall some small detail from his busy, brilliant mind. 'There is something I need to address with him first...'

'It was his mother's funeral last week,' Emma responded. She knew because she had arranged the flowers and condolences that had been sent on behalf of D'Amato Financiers.

'That's right.' He nodded brief thanks—he would start the difficult meeting with some friendly conversation, before heading for the jugular. It wasn't actually a tactic, Emma had realised after a few weeks of working for him.

Luca could separate the business side of things from the social with alarming ease—his condolences would be genuine, his sympathy real, but when it came down to business there would be no concessions or momentary reprieves—which was why D'Amato Financiers were not just surviving but thriving. Luca dealt in money, serious money—his own and other people's—and, eternally vigilant, he pre-empted things with skill and ease.

And he was pre-empting now as she glanced at her watch.

'HR can wait,' Luca said. 'This is important.'

Kasumi, Mr Hirosiko's PA, was always sweet and unruffled whenever Emma had dealings with her, and this morning she was smiling into the screen when Emma finally found the right button to push. She chatted for a moment with the other woman, admiring her glossy blue-black hair in the video conferencing room as she arranged Luca's meeting desk and pulled up some figures he had asked for on his laptop.

'I will tell Mr Hirosiko that Mr D'Amato is ready for him,' Kasumi said when both women were sure everything was in order. And though she had done this many times now, there was still an awkwardness talking to the large screen, still a certain awkwardness in Emma's movements as she set up the room.

'*Konbanwa,*' Emma said, wishing Kasumi a good evening.

On Luca's instructions she had been learning Japanese in what could loosely be called her spare time. On the drive to work or to visit her father she practised the difficult language with some CDs Luca had lent her—but after six weeks she was still on level one!

'Have a pleasant day,' Kasumi returned the greeting, but as Luca strode into the room, Emma realised that the calm, unruffled Kasumi wasn't impervious to his charms either. On the vast screen above the meeting room Emma watched as the other woman's pale cheeks turned pink—and who could blame her? Luca didn't just stride into the meeting room and bid her a brief good morning. No, he walked in and stood and gave her his full attention, bade her good morning and chatted in rather impressive Japanese, managing to keep full-on eye contact that would make any woman squirm—and then he treated Kasumi to one of his rare laughs.

'And that, I'm afraid, is as far as I can go!'

'You did very well.' Kasumi smiled. 'Your Japanese is improving.'

'A bit,' Luca agreed. Walking to his desk and seeing Emma's slightly rigid lips, he turned back to the screen, catching Kasumi's waiting eyes again as thick heat flared in Emma's throat. *'Saifu o otoshimashita,'* Luca said, and Kasumi started to giggle. *'Isha o yonde kudasai,'* he added, to Kasumi's obvious delight, and Emma was appalled at the prickles that rose on the back of her neck, at her indignation at their obvious flirting while she was in the room. Well, she wouldn't show it, of course; instead, she poured his water and checked that the meeting was being recorded, as no doubt Luca offered promises of dinner and breakfast in bed on his next trip to Japan, or whatever it was that was making Kasumi giggle so.

Still, the skittish giggles from the, oh, so professional Kasumi soon faded as her boss entered the room, but it was Emma's cheeks that were still flaming even after she discreetly left the meeting room.

'Everything okay?' Evelyn checked as Emma collected some files for the rescheduled HR meeting.

'Everything's fine,' Emma said, forcing a smile, only everything wasn't fine. She was unsettled, restless—angry even—and she didn't want to acknowledge why. Taking her chair in the meeting, she eyed the pale pink blooms of an impressive display of orchids—Luca's choice of flowers for the week—her teeth grinding against each other as she choked on that alien emotion. It was jealousy that had flared when he had spoken with Kasumi, and it had no place in her life.

He was a rake, a born flirt, a serial heart-breaker and a self-confessed playboy. He'd crush her in the palm of his hand. Well, Kasumi was welcome to him—they all were. She'd been right to say no to his ridiculous offer. If she accepted it, well, her job would be as good as over. Whatever Luca had implied about nothing sexual happening between them while they were away, Emma didn't believe it for a second. And Luca didn't like looking at his mistakes afterwards. Evelyn had warned her of that from the beginning.

Yes, she'd been right, but then why at night did she lie there thinking, wishing it could be different, wishing she could pluck up the courage to say yes?

Her head buzzing from the HR meeting, she returned to find several personal calls that needed to be returned—and not one of them brought her joy.

The interested vendor that had been through

her house at the weekend had put in a bid—on a different house.

And, though he insisted he wanted to help, her brother Rory had just found out that his child maintenance to his ex-wife had been increased, so, sorry, no, he couldn't.

'Rory!' Emma snapped. 'We agreed when we chose this home for Dad that we'd cover the fees between us until the house sold!'

'That was before we found out how much of a mortgage Dad had on the house. Look, Em, even if the house does sell, it's not going to keep him there for ever. He's only in his sixties. I've been talking with the boys and maybe we should look for somewhere cheaper...'

They'd do it, too.

As Emma hung up on her brother, she knew without a doubt that they'd do it—would move him from a home where he was, for the most part, happy, if it meant they could get their hands on some cash.

And then the nursing home rang to say that her father had been asking for her all morning.

'He's fine,' the nurse assured her. 'Just a touch anxious...'

'Look, I know I haven't been in as much recently.' Emma closed her eyes in exhaustion. 'It's not that I don't want to.'

'We're not trying to make you feel guilty,' the nurse said. 'You asked that we keep you up to date, and though he is confused, well...he does notice that you're not visiting as often as you were.'

'Tell him that I'll be in soon,' Emma said.

'Can I tell him when?'

They didn't mean to make her feel guilty— except guilty was exactly how she felt.

And at times it was completely overwhelming.

She pressed her fingers into her eyes in a bid to stem the tears, stem the urge to just throw in the towel, to let her brothers sort out the mess. To stop caring about a father who had treated her so poorly in the past.

When the house did sell, she'd be homeless. Oh, the profits from the sale would cover the overdue fees of the home, but it was the backlog of debt that was giving her nightmares.

'Problem?' Emma jumped, unsure how long Luca had been watching her.

'Not at all…' She forced a smile. 'The meeting went well; I'll write up a report and get the information to you.'

'I wasn't talking about the HR meeting.' Luca frowned. 'Is anything wrong?'

'Nothing,' Emma said, then realising what he'd seen she relented. 'I've got a bit of headache, that's all.'

'My housekeeper's not well.'

'Oh!' Emma blinked, reaching for the phone. 'Did you want me to ring the agency and arrange a replacement?'

'I'll survive for a day,' Luca said magnanimously, 'but I *am* going to be flying to Japan this afternoon. Evelyn's coming with me, she's gone home to get ready, so can you go over to my apartment and pack for me?'

It was a strange byproduct, Emma had realised, of being rich and in demand—there was very little personal in his personal life. There was a whole army of people ensuring that every minute of his valuable time was put to best use. Letting herself into his vast, luxurious apartment a little later, Emma bent down and went to stroke Pepper, who duly growled a warning, then waddled to the huge glass sliding door to be let out. Emma wandered out onto the balcony and stared at the spectacular view of the Thames, before setting to work. She headed into the bedroom, opening her organiser and locating the list that would tell her what was required for a two-night international business trip.

All the information was there in her folder.

His immaculate suits and shoes were packed, as was his equally immaculate casual wear, and then she opened his underwear drawer to see neat rows of folded hipsters and socks as if they were on display in an exclusive store. There was nothing personal about the choices she made—the list saw to that. These cufflinks were preferred with this tie and shirt, these shoes with that suit… It just felt personal, that was all.

'Hey!' Emma jumped as Luca walked into the bedroom unannounced, blushing as she held a handful of his hipsters. It just seemed wrong somehow to be going through his underwear drawer, even though it was her job to be in there.

He was completely at ease with it, of course.

Just kicked off his shoes and lay on the bed, chatting on his phone as Emma walked through to the sumptuous bathroom to pack his toiletries and to try and not listen as he made a couple of personal calls—cancelling his plans for the next couple of nights and, by the sound of it, breaking a couple of hearts in the process.

'Why?' Luca asked as she came back into the bedroom with his toiletry bag and was finishing off his packing, 'when I say I'm going to Japan, do they think it has something to do with them—why would they think that I'm lying?'

'Because you usually are,' Emma pointed out.

'Well, I'm not this time.' He ran lazy eyes over her, taking in the smudges under her eyes, the vague distraction that slightly displaced her more usual sunny nature. 'What's wrong, Em?'

'Ms Stephenson to you!' Emma instantly pulled him up, refusing, just refusing as she always did with him, to cross the line. 'But you can call me Emma.'

'What's wrong, Emma? And don't give me that rubbish about a headache.'

'Nothing's wrong,' Emma insisted.

He lay back on the bed, closed his eyes and gave a low laugh.

'Now that I've stopped, I realise I have a headache too!"

He did—right there at the front of his head. He could hear the sounds of her packing, and it would be so incredibly easy to just close his eyes and sleep. He didn't want to go to Tokyo. Incredibly, and not for the first time lately, he could hardly stomach the thought of the flight.

'We should *fare force…*' Luca smiled with his eyes still closed.

'Sorry?'

'You know...' he waved his hand, tried to come up with the English word for it, but it eluded him, and those gorgeous navy eyes finally opened to hers. 'Leave school...' He snapped his fingers, impatient with himself now. 'Not go back.'

'Play hooky!' Emma grinned.

'Play hooky!' Luca smiled at the term and closed his eyes. 'That would be good—we could get ice-packs from the fridge for our foreheads and lie in the dark and ignore the phone.'

'Sounds good.'

'And I wasn't being inappropriate.'

'I know.' Emma smiled, because she knew exactly what he meant, exactly how he felt, because she felt it too. 'But we can't.'

He looked as if he was dozing, except his mind was actually whirring.

He was sick of keeping things businesslike between them.

He was cross with himself too for his handling of things.

He wanted her.

And yet he didn't—because he actually liked working with her. Liked having her around, and once things moved, as they surely would, well…

There was no question of a future for them.

Not even a hint of one.

He deliberately didn't do long-term relation-ships—as soon as things got too comfortable, too nice, he cut all ties.

It was a promise he had made himself many years ago.

He lay there, head pounding, listened to her pad out to the kitchen, to the running of the tap, and for once he was torn with indecision.

He wanted her.

He didn't want to lose her.

Yet he couldn't have both.

'Here.' She was back, holding out a glass of water and punching out two tablets from a blister pack. 'Take these.'

'Only if you do.'

Emma punched out two for herself and they shared the glass of water. Funny that he noticed a little thing like that—funny that to Luca it mattered that she didn't go and get another glass.

'We'll feel better in twenty minutes.' Emma smiled, glad that they seemed to be talking normally again after the strain of the past few weeks. 'It says so on the box.'

She zipped his suit holder and picked up the phone to summon his driver as Luca downed a quick shot of espresso from his coffee machine. He stuffed files and papers into his briefcase as he gave her a few last-minute instructions that would take about a couple of hours to execute.

'Any problems, ring Kasumi. It doesn't matter what time it is there—things have to be in place for tomorrow.'

'Sure!' He watched her bristle slightly at the mention of the other PA's name and inside Luca smiled.

'*Saifu o otoshimashita,*' Luca said, watching her cheeks go pink as he repeated the words he had said to Kasumi. '*Isha o yonde kudasai.*'

'You can tell her yourself when you see her,' Emma responded coolly.

'I've dropped my wallet!' Luca laughed. 'Can someone please call a doctor? I was practising new phrases!'

He made her laugh, but her little flare of jealousy was acknowledged and out there now—and she didn't know how to handle him, or this energy that swirled between them. His dangerous offer still dangled in the air and right there at that moment she wanted to reach out and grab it. Maybe she could fake it, Emma thought wildly, maybe she could pretend that she wasn't a virgin. Maybe her body would just *know* what to do. Evelyn buzzed and he picked up his briefcase. 'Don't bother going back to the office,' he said, nodding to a PC. 'Do it from here and then finish up for the day...' He frowned at her pale face. 'Actually, have tomorrow off.'

'I've got a full schedule tomorrow.'

'Cancel it—my orders.' Luca shrugged. 'Have a day off and sort out whatever "nothing" is, or, failing that, catch up on some sleep. I'll see you on Monday.'

And as always, he left home as easily as he left a hotel room—just turned and walked out of the door without a second thought.

As he handed his driver his bag, her voice reached him. 'Have a safe trip.'

He looked back over his shoulder, a throw-away comment, a rushed farewell on the tip of his tongue, and in that moment he glimpsed it.

Leaving.

How it *could* feel to leave home.

'See you Monday.' His voice was gruff and Emma stood there as he closed the door behind him.

Now that he was gone, she breathed.

She wanted to tell him.

For the first time ever, she actually wanted to confide in someone—to tell him what 'nothing' meant. To share, to reveal, not that he might fix it, because she knew no one could do that, not so he might wave a magic wand and make her father suddenly better, or the nursing-home fees smaller, or the anger at her father's past treatment of her disappear. It was none of that. No, standing in that bedroom, seeing him lying on the bed, those dark blue eyes concerned, all she had wanted was to do exactly what Luca had said.

Fare force.

To escape for a little while, to lie down beside him in a dark room and let the world carry right on without her for a little while.

As the door flung open again she stood to attention almost, snapped the smile back on her face as Luca hurried in and strode across the lounge towards her. He must have forgotten his passport or phone or…

And then it happened.

What she had been secretly thinking about from the very first time she had seen him.

What she had desperately been trying to avoid and ignore.

That bubbling, simmering tension between them finally acknowledged.

His arms pulling her in and his mouth pressing on hers.

Wrapping her in his embrace and crushing her with his mouth.

And it should have been unexpected, should have caused shock, anger, except it was just pure relief.

Sheer, sheer relief to be kissed and to kiss back.

His tongue was cool and he tasted of mint and man and coffee and escape—and Emma didn't at that point question it. All she did was feel it. The bliss of firm lips and the scent that had always made itself known captivated her as it intensified in their close proximity.

His body to touch was everything her eyes had promised—lean and powerful beneath her hands and against her own body.

His eyes were closed, she *had* to look, had to see him, and it made her want this moment more because he was as lost in it as she. He moved from her mouth, his moist lips lingering on her cheeks, his hands on the small of her back pushing her hips into his, and then it was her ear he was kissing. Instead of moving her head away, with *his* kiss, she leaned towards him, curved into his touch, weaker in her body as Luca's mouth met her throat and thoroughly kissed it too—her neck was arching and his hands had moved, both now on the peach of her buttocks and pressing her heat into him. Then his mouth found hers again and she tasted his ragged breaths—and it was just like the first time she'd ever seen him, because the world was black again, everything diminished and nothing else mattered, just his kiss and his body. And who cared where it might lead or the damage it might do, because for the first time ever she wasn't thinking or fixing or solving or surviving—she was living, just alive and alert, but only for this, for him, for them.

And then the intercom buzzed—Evelyn warning him they would be late.

'That,' Emma said in a shaky voice as he pulled back from her, 'didn't just happen.' She put her fingers up to her lips, could feel them swollen and tasting of him, and what had been simple and natural a moment ago was suddenly very confusing.

And then he kissed her again.

'Or that,' Luca said, and he stared into her lovely clear eyes and saw the whir of confusion. She was wholly adorable and for a second he felt regret.

Real, wretched regret, because soon he'd have to get used to missing her.

But it was too late for regret, because he'd pulled the pin now and the countdown to the inevitable end had started.

As Evelyn's voice on the intercom filled the room, warning she was on her way up, he gave Emma a quick frantic look that made her giggle. 'Don't tell her!'

'God, no…' Emma swallowed. 'Just go…' She was more than confused now, trying to assert herself, wishing she could turn back the clock, only Luca was upping the ante now.

'Think about Italy.' He was still holding her, his kiss this steam that wouldn't evaporate. She felt as if she'd been running, could feel her hammering heartbeat and the dampness between her legs. His knowing eyes were on hers, his hands on her hips, and he pulled her a little way in towards him once more, giving her just another small, decadent feel of what was there waiting there for her if only she could reach out and take it.

'What are you so scared of?' Luca asked, and after just a moment's thought she gave him a very honest answer.

'Losing.' She stared back at him, and it wasn't just the job, or the jet-set lifestyle, she was scared of losing, but him. 'Let's just forget that it happened.'

Futile words—and they both knew it.

CHAPTER SEVEN

'DAD, please don't cry.'

He always got upset when it was time for her to leave. She hadn't got to the nursing home till eight p.m., and so couldn't stay, but Luca left for Sicily tomorrow—he had finally agreed to stay with his family for a few nights so at least for a couple of days she'd be able to see more of her father.

It was worth it—even if her boss was barely talking to her! Luca was clearly smarting as, even after their kiss, she still had persisted in saying no to accompanying him to his sister's wedding.

'I just miss her…' Frank was staring at a photo of her mother and Emma just didn't get it—growing up, it had been practically forbidden to talk about her, and now it was practically all he talked about! Going over the past as if it had happened just yesterday, and it actually hurt to hear it. 'I just want my Gloria. Why did she have to leave us?'

'Dad, she didn't want to…'

'Off with that scum of a man…calling himself an artist! How could she walk out on her family?' Emma felt the blood in her veins turn to ice.

'She didn't walk out on us, Dad, she was killed in a car accident.'

'Out on the town with her fancy man, leaving her little girl crying at home,' Frank sobbed, and the night nurse came in then.

'We're going to give him his sleeping tablet now, Emma, and settle him down.'

'How could she walk out on four kids?'

How she wanted to press him for answers, to bombard him with questions, but the nurse was giving him his medicine, trying to settle him down, and he was just too frail and too confused to push it right then.

'Rory!' She didn't care if it was late, or that she was driving, she punched in his name and waited for him to pick up, not bothering to introduce herself, just blurting out her question. 'Did Mum walk out on us?'

'Emma?'

'Just tell me what happened.'

'You know what happened,' Rory sighed. 'There was a car accident.'

'Who was driving?'

Emma knew he was holding back, could tell by the uncomfortable pause before Rory next spoke.

'What's Dad saying now?'

'That she walked out on us.'

There was a very long silence and then came a truth she had never prepared for. 'Mum left us a month before she died.' As he heard her start to sob, Rory showed rare concern for his sister. 'Look, pull over, you shouldn't be driving...'

'She just *left* us!'

'She wanted to "find herself", do her damned art, see this new guy. Look, it was twenty years ago! I don't see what you're getting so worked up about,' Rory attempted. 'It doesn't change anything.'

Oh, but it did.

She clicked off the phone and threw it onto the passenger seat.

It changed *everything*.

She shouldn't be driving in this state…so she forced herself to concentrate, forced herself to be calm until she pulled up to her family home—the for-sale sign on the door, the home, the family her mother had walked out on—and only then did she see him. His car was there, waiting for her, and Luca climbed out of the back seat and walked towards her. His face was grey, and in the streetlight she could see the tiny lines around his eyes, the dark, weary shadows beneath them.

She could smell the whisky on his breath and hear the dread in his words, and it matched her soul.

'Come with me tomorrow.' He didn't touch her, he didn't make any demands, he didn't even ask, he just matched her need.

'Yes.'

He blinked just a touch at the ease of her answer, a smile spreading over his face, relief creeping in, because *now* he could stomach it, *now* he could face it.

'What took you so long?' Luca asked.

Her mother had left them...

This idol she had looked up to, the perfect woman, gone too soon, had feet of clay after all—and she was angry, but boy it felt good to contemplate living instead of mourning, to let go of the past and dive into the future.

And there it was—if only she had the nerve to reach out and take it.

'I've never slept with anyone before.' She watched his reaction, saw his eyes widen, and thought it was almost fear that darted across his features. 'Don't worry, Luca,' she said before he could respond, 'I haven't been waiting for Mr Right to come along and relieve me of my virginity.'

'Emma!' He hadn't bargained on this. Not

once, not for a second had he considered this. He wanted relief, distraction, and instead this was responsibility, but Emma just laughed and kissed his cheek. She was in a strange, slightly manic mood he didn't understand, but it was actually a little bit catching. 'You know I'm not looking for serious…'

'I know the rules, Luca.' Emma's voice was steady. 'And I'm prepared to play by them. Now, if you'll excuse me, I have a weekend away to pack for.'

As his private jet lifted into the early morning sky, all Emma wanted to do was close her eyes and sleep.

The night had been spent packing and planning and then dreading, and finally weeping.

Weeping for a woman she didn't know at all, for a father she had always resented but was maybe, just maybe starting to understand.

She was resilient, though, she had always had to be, so she hid her swollen eyes behind huge sunglasses and pleaded another headache when Luca commented on them. She had, after a night of weeping, pushed away yesterday's news and was in a bizarre way actually glad to be getting away for a few days and leaving it all behind her.

They were served a sumptuous breakfast, pastries, waffles, meats and the thick treacly coffee Luca survived on, but Emma wasn't hungry and Luca watched her push her food around her plate and frowned over his newspaper.

There was something different about her. Oh, she was chatty and polite, only there was a vague distraction about her, a restlessness almost, something he couldn't quite pinpoint.

Her acceptance yesterday had floored him.

He had engineered this weekend—had been hoping the mutual attraction between them would be quickly sated, that she would be the solace that would get him through the difficult time ahead.

He had been dreading the wedding for months now—back to the family home, back to his father and uncles. Emma was to have been his relief.

But not now, and he had only himself to blame.

Breaking hearts he could deal with.

But breaking hers…he was having serious second thoughts about that.

He saw that she wasn't eating her food and, remembering her beverage of choice when she was flagging, ordered his crew to fetch it for her. Then he sat and watched closely as she took a grateful sip of thick hot chocolate.

'You have brothers, yes?' Luca checked, watching a small furrow emerge on her brow.

'Three,' she acknowledged briefly.

'And what happened with your mother?'

'I really don't want to talk about it…'

'But we have to,' he insisted. He finished with his breakfast and pushed his plate away. It was removed instantly, the conversation continuing when the steward had discreetly disappeared. 'You speak little of your personal life.'

'The hours I work hardly allow for much of a personal life!' she protested.

'Emma, for this weekend you are supposed to

be my girlfriend—I am taking you to meet my parents. Surely you can see that I ought to know some of your background.'

He had a point. In the weeks she had known him, she had been privy to all sorts of information about him.

His diary had noted birthdays, anniversaries, his clothing preferences for the times when he needed an outfit at short notice, even the hairdresser he used for his regular trim. She knew, because it had been her job to hire a new housekeeper for him, how he liked things done, the sort of food he kept at home—had even downloaded some songs for him—so if she were put on the spot right now, she knew enough about Luca to bluff her way through, whereas apart from the fact her father was in a nursing home, Luca knew practically nothing about her.

That was the way she had wanted it.

But, as Luca pointed out, their stories needed to tally. She screwed up her courage, and then suddenly he came up with a compromise.

'Okay—I'll tell my mother you don't like talking about it.'

'About what?' she asked, bewildered.

'Anything I don't know the answer to,' he said, pleased that he'd managed to eke out a smile from her. 'We have been seeing each other for a couple of months,' Luca said, 'since you came and worked for me. We have both decided that working together is too much, so you will be finishing up soon.'

'To do what?'

Luca shrugged—trying to think what his girlfriends actually did all day.

'Modelling?'

'Please!' Emma snorted with laughter. 'If I'm to convincingly play the part of your devoted girlfriend, then at least there has to be a semblance of me in there. So…' She chewed on her lip and tried to imagine a world where this man loved her, tried for the first time to actually picture a world with herself and Luca as a couple, and glimpsed the impossible—being the sole recipient of his affection.

Yet even if it was impossible, it was still fun pretending.

'I'm applying to study art, you're organising a studio for me in your apartment, in that big room at the back that you don't use. It's supposed to be a surprise, but unbeknown to you I've guessed.'

'Are you good?' Luca asked. 'At art?'

'I've just started night school. My dad didn't like me pursuing...' Her voice faded for a moment, realising now why he might have hated that side of her so, but she refused to dwell on it, it was just too big to deal with right now. 'Oh, and by the way...' She gave him a wry smile. 'Just in case it comes up in the conversation, today's my birthday.'

'Really?' Luca frowned. 'You should have said.'

'I just did.'

'I am sorry to pull you away from your celebrations.'

'You didn't,' Emma answered tartly. 'It's really no big deal.'

'And how old is Emma today?'

'She's twenty-five!' It made her blush to say it, with the information she'd so recently given him. She saw just the slight rise of one eyebrow, but thankfully he chose not to comment.

'So what about you?' she asked.

'You know about me.'

'I don't know much about your family.'

'My mother is Mia, my father is Rico. He was a policeman, and you know about Daniela…'

'And he's sick…' Emma probed. 'Your father?'

'Very.'

'And you don't get on?'

He gave a tight shrug and clearly it was Luca now who didn't want to talk about it!

'Anything else I should know?' she pressed.

'Nothing.' Luca shrugged. 'As I said, my father was the village policeman, I went to boarding school from ten…' He saw her frown at that. 'That is usual where I come from, as the school in the village only goes up that age. It was all pretty normal really.'

'Till their son became a billionaire.' Emma

smiled, but then she was serious. 'Why, Luca? Why do you hate them so—?'

'Not Daniela,' he interrupted. 'And not my mother...' He shook his head. 'Let's just do what we have to, smile, enjoy, *familia*...' He sneered the word. 'Let's just get through it.'

There was a bedroom at the rear of the plane, but for the relatively short flight to Italy he just tipped back his seat and stretched out and Emma did the same. Hoping her swollen eyes had settled, she took off her glasses and lay back.

'I love these chairs,' Emma commented. 'I wish I had one at home.'

She squirmed in comfort as the attendant placed a soft warmed blanket over her.

'If I ever have to bribe you I'll remember that.' Then he added, 'Are you okay?' when it took her a second too long to smile.

'I'm fine.'

'Because if you're worried about what you told me yesterday—' he was direct as always '—well, you don't have to be—I'm not in anything for the long haul, and...' he gave a slightly wistful smile '...if you've waited this long for it to be right, I do understand.'

'I'm not upset about that,' Emma said, because right now she wasn't—Luca had wanted a fling and actually so now did she. She probably wasn't very good fling material, but she'd deal with it. It really was good to just get away.

'Then what *are* you so upset about?' They were lying flat, facing each other. 'You look as if you've been crying.'

'Not about you,' she retorted.

'Good,' Luca said, and he intended to keep it that way. 'Here.' He dug in his pocket and pulled out a black box and handed it to her as if it were a sweet. 'You'd better put these on— if we were going out, I would have bought you nice gifts.'

'Goodness!' Emma gasped and held up two earrings, the huge teardrop diamonds sparkling. 'They look so real.'

'They *are* real,' Luca said dryly.

'I'd better not lose them then.' She tried to sound as casual as him, but it felt strange to be holding his gift, strange to be lying beside him and very hard not to imagine that this was...

Real.

So she thought about other things instead. Silly things—like she used to when she was a child and couldn't sleep, not the grown-up things that she thought of now.

The steward clipped belts loosely around them and on leaving them dimmed the lights. Luca closed his eyes, but smiled when she carried on talking.

'It's like being in an ambulance.'

'Have you ever been in an ambulance?'

'No,' Emma admitted, but that didn't deter her. 'I'm in a coma, but I can hear, though no one knows it, and everyone I've ever fancied is going to dash to my bedside and beg me not to die, and say that they love me really.'

'What are you talking about?' He turned his head to face her again.

'Don't you do that?' Emma blinked. 'Make up stories before you go to sleep?'

'No.'

'What do you do?' she asked curiously.

'I close my eyes…' he shrugged '…and I go to sleep.'

'Just like that?'

'So long as there is no one talking.'

He'd wondered what to expect—if she'd be miserable, angry, but instead she was just being Emma.

He was glad that she was there.

He could feel the familiar knot of tension tighten in his stomach as the plane sliced through the sky—the same knot he felt every time he came home, the same sick dread he had felt coming home from boarding school on the holidays.

The same sick dread he had felt every night as he had lain in bed as a child.

Luca breathed out, suddenly needing to swallow, sweat beading on his forehead as he willed sleep to come.

His father was old and weak and dying, there was surely nothing to dread now.

And then he saw it.

Like a dog dashing into the street, his mind swerved to avoid it, but his father's fist was there, slamming into his mother's face, the image so violent, so real it was as if his father's fist had made contact with his own.

He jumped.

That horrible jump where you woke up with heart racing, only Luca knew that he hadn't been asleep.

'Luca?' Emma murmured. She was almost asleep, though, he could tell from her voice, and knew because in her right mind Emma would never reach out and hold his hand.

It felt like weakness to take it.

But it helped, it actually helped.

CHAPTER EIGHT

'WELCOME to our home.'

Landing at Palermo, Emma had enjoyed the helicopter ride that had taken them on the final leg of their journey to his small coastal village—and everywhere Emma looked the view was stunning. Houses perched on top of houses all staring out to the twinkling Mediterranean, and Luca's family home was the jewel in the crown—the basic home had been lavishly extended, and every room was angled to take in the spectacular sea view.

Luca's mother's welcome was warm and effusive, pulling Emma into an embrace and kissing her on both cheeks, then guiding her through to a large terrace that ran the length of the house while chatting non-stop in her rich accent, alternating between English and Italian.

'Luca!' The squeals of delight from Daniela had Emma smiling, and he was far more pleased to see his sister than Emma's own brothers ever were—hugging her warmly, teasing her about the face pack she was wearing and introducing her to Emma, who Daniela eyed with the same suspicious navy eyes as her brother, but she smiled and chatted in very good English, before drifting back to her bedroom to get ready for her big day.

'*Dove Pa?*' Luca asked.

'*Dorme,*' Mia said, and then translated for Emma. 'He sleeps... Oh!' She gave a warm smile as her husband entered. Tall and thin, his once raven hair peppered with silver, he would have cut an imposing figure in his time.

'Luca!' He embraced his son, kissed him on the cheek as was the Italian way. Luca briefly hugged him back, but Emma could feel the sudden tension in the room. '*Comesta?*'

'This is Emma.' Luca's voice was just a touch

short as he introduced her to his father. Despite Rico's fragility he took her firmly by the hands, kissing her on the cheeks and welcoming her to the family…making a kissing gesture with his fingers when he saw the impressive earrings, which made Mia laugh.

'Come, Rico…' She plumped the cushions on what must be his seat and fussed over him as he lowered his tall frame. Emma stood, suddenly awkward as Luca just watched, his face an impassive mask Emma couldn't interpret.

'Luca is upset.' As Emma did the right thing and helped his mother prepare coffee in the kitchen, finally there was an explanation for his strange lack of reaction. 'It is hard for him to see his father so ill. It is almost a year since Luca was here, it would be difficult for him to see the changes.'

'Of course.' Emma set up the tiny coffee cups on saucers and it should have appeased her, except it didn't. Luca had his own plane—his own travel team for heaven's sake, and even her selfish brothers managed a visit to their father once a month—there was surely a lot more behind this *familia* that kept Luca away so coolly.

It was a busy house. The drinks and pastries that had been set up were not just for Luca and Emma's benefit, but for an endless parade of guests, all wanting to meet Luca's girlfriend and to wish Daniela well for her big day. And Luca saw the strain showing in Emma's smiling face as the shadows lengthened, and he was proud of her, proud at how easy she had made it for him to be here, and he wanted to make it easier for her too.

'I thought I might take Emma out for dinner. I know you are busy…'

There were protests from Mia, of course, but not too many. Rico was tired and wanted to get back to his bed, and Daniela was calling for help from the bedroom. Just a typical family two days before a wedding, and, as pleasant as the afternoon had been, it was rather nice to get out.

They walked through his village, the scent of the sea filling the late summer sky, and he took her to a local restaurant. No matter how many

Italian restaurants she had been to before, nothing could compare to the simple fare of fresh pasta swished in basil pesto and lavishly smothered in Parmesan. The wine was rich and deep and fruity, and they sat outside drinking it, bathed in citronella-fragranced candlelight. Though they had eaten out together on many occasions, both in London and abroad, this was nothing like a business dinner, because here no business was discussed.

Her eyes were huge in the candlelight, her laughter infectious, and for the first time at home Luca relaxed, till the conversation turned personal.

'So you brought Martha here…' She took a sip of her wine rather than look at him.

'It was a bad idea,' Luca finally admitted. 'Martha insisted it would change nothing.'

'But it did?'

'My family assumed we were serious—and then Martha started believing it too.'

'Is it so impossible?' Emma blinked. 'You talk as if you've no intention of *ever* settling down.'

'I don't,' Luca said. 'I would grow bored, restless...I would rather have my pick.' He gave her a smile. 'Italian men get *better* looking as they get older, so I don't think I'll be short of company.'

And it was honest, so why did it hurt her?

The thought of him in years to come, that jet hair dashed with silver, his distinguished features slightly more ravaged—this beautiful man walking the planet alone...yes, she couldn't deny that it hurt.

'I'm surprised you haven't built a hotel here, if you don't like staying with your family.' Emma refused to get morose.

'It is often suggested by developers, but it would ruin it. There are natural springs close by, so it would certainly be a tourist paradise, but...' Luca shook his head. 'No.' He had no desire to be here any more than he had to and no desire to discuss his family further, so he concentrated on their meal instead. 'There are two desserts,' Luca translated the menu for her. 'Tiramisu or tiramisu with cream...'

He liked it that she laughed, liked it that she didn't decline dessert and instead ordered it with cream, liked eating with a woman who actually enjoyed it!

'They make it once a week, and each night they soak in a little more liquor, so by Friday it has reached perfection,' he told her.

'Then thank God it's Friday.' She smiled.

She had tasted many tiramisus—good and bad, tiramisu ice cream, tiramisu from the supermarket, even tiramisu from an expensive Italian restaurant Luca had taken her to with clients, but as the sweet moist dessert met her mouth Emma realised she had never *really* tasted tiramisu.

'It's gorgeous.' She closed her eyes and relished it for a moment.

And so are you, Luca thought, watching her.

She could feel his eyes on her, and dashed to the ladies to touch up her make-up, wrestled with underwear that was supposed to smooth out bumps and realised that maybe the tiramisu was more potent than it looked as she struggled to replace the top on her lip gloss.

Or she'd had too much wine with dinner, Emma thought, staring at her glittering eyes and rosy cheeks.

Or maybe it was just a reaction to the company!

Even if it wasn't real, it was so good to be away, to forget, to be twenty-five years old today and go out for dinner with the sexiest man in the world.

He signed for the bill and they wandered back, taking the sandy route. Emma slipped off her sandals, feeling a million miles from London, from everything, as her feet sank into the wet sand, and her ankles were bathed by the warm sea.

'How can you bear to stay away?' she murmured.

'You eventually get tired of the view,' Luca said, 'no matter how beautiful.'

'I meant from your family.'

'You've seen my schedule.' Luca shrugged, and then expanded a little. 'I ring, I send money, I try to get back when I can…' He knew it sounded lame, knew she thought him a selfish person, and that was completely fine with him.

They stopped walking, Luca picking up a handful of stones and skimming them out to sea, looking out at the rolling waves and the high crescent of a new moon. He relented a touch about his family—he told himself it was because he didn't want to kill the mood, but…she *was* nice to talk to. 'It's not just the view you get tired of—but the place, the people, the unspoken rules…'

'Rules?'

'*Familia.*' There was a scathing note to his voice. 'Everything is for appearances' sake— that is why I am here, remember! What *will* people think if the brother, the only son, just drops in for the wedding? That is the type of question you hear all the time as you grow up. They are so worried about how they appear, what people will think. There is shame that their only son has not settled down. Every time I come home, it's always the same questions…'

'And that's enough to keep you away?' She didn't buy it. 'A few questions?'

'You see a frail old man near death, Emma.' She felt the prickles on the back of her neck rise as he continued, 'And the village sees the patriarch of the D'Amato family, close to the end of a good and rich life...'

'What do *you* see, Luca?' she asked quietly.

'My mother's fear.' If it was only a hundredth of it, it was still more than he'd ever admitted to anyone, and there was this curl of trepidation in his stomach as for the first time he broke the D'Amato code of silence. 'How, even when he can hardly walk, she still jumps when he enters a room, still laughs too loudly at his jokes...'

'Was he violent towards her?' Emma asked.

'A bit.' His guard shot back up. 'Yet he is weak and pathetic now—there is nothing more to fear.'

'Is that why you stay away?'

Luca shrugged, a bit guilty now, embarrassed perhaps at admitting so much, and he tried to laugh it off. 'Apparently I should have married some

sweet virgin, produced several children by now—
no matter whether or not it makes me happy.'

'But you haven't,' Emma pointed out.

'Because there are no more virgins—no good-
looking ones anyway.' His mouth curved into a
smile at his own joke and then, appalled, he remembered. 'Emma, I'm sorry!' He had to run to
catch up with her. 'I forgot, okay?'

'Just leave it.' She shrugged him off, angry,
annoyed, embarrassed and very, very close to
tears. She was sick of it, sick of it, sick of it!

'Hey.' He caught her hand and spun her
around. 'I'm sorry if I offended you—I just
never thought—'

'No, you didn't!' Emma flared.

'You're not ugly…you're gorgeous,' Luca attempted, 'and the guy who gets you will be a
lucky man indeed.' Huge green eyes looked up
at him. 'I'm just not sure that should be me…'
He stared at the oh, so, familiar beach, dragged
in the familiar smells, and though he so desperately wanted her, he didn't actually *have* to have

her—there was sweet relief in just her company tonight and the knowing that she would be beside him tonight.

'Even if I *want* it to be you?'

'Emma...' He didn't finish so they walked on in silence, and it was Luca who finally broke it. 'Come on, let's get home. I'll text Ma and let her know.' Which to Emma seemed a strange thing for a thirty-four-year-old playboy to do, but she was too upset about how the night had turned out, and really never gave it another thought, especially when they stepped into a house that was in darkness.

'They must have gone to bed,' Luca said, and then the lights snapped on.

'Surprise!' She saw the usually deadpan Luca grinning at her stunned reaction, as shouts of 'Happy birthday' and *'Tanti auguiri'* rang out, and slowly the realisation set in that this was all for her.

Luca could never have known how much this might mean to her, how completely overwhelming this was, because there were gifts all prettily wrapped and a table set with glasses and liqueurs and, centre stage, a cake. A huge sponge filled with cream and iced on top and in shaky handwriting the words *Tanti Auguiri Emma.*

Her first birthday cake, her first birthday party—well, at least, the first she could remember.

'Sorry,' Mia said. 'Rico wanted to stay up but he was tired.' Emma could see the mood in the house was actually better without him, and then Mia apologised that the cake was homemade, which made Emma's eyes well up. 'Luca only told me yesterday, there was no time to order one—and—'

'Yesterday?' Her head whipped around to him—that he had known all along, before she'd even told him, and that he had thought to ring ahead and arrange all this for her...

'Did you really think I'd forget your birthday?'

She opened her gifts—first a stunning white lace nightdress from Mia. 'For your trousseau,' she hinted. There was some body lotion and perfume from Daniela, and from Luca a silver charm bracelet, with a diamond-studded 'E' and a pretty horoscope charm, The Virgo Lady, dangling on her bracelet, which he'd bought before he'd known she really was one!

Did everything lead there?

'Emma wanted to start a charm bracelet collection,' Luca said as he snapped it on her wrist and kissed her trembling mouth, and she wondered at what a convincing lover he made.

'Then we will know what to get you at Christmas.' Mia smiled and it was too much— the unexpected kindness, the care, the cake and the fact that there would be no family Christmas, that none of this was real...

Tiny thoughts, like flickering stars were there on the periphery of her mind, and she was almost scared to focus on them in case they flared.

Cakes and presents and the love that her mother had denied her. Yet a thousand miles from home and with people she didn't know, it wasn't the time to be exploring her feelings, so again she squashed them down, plastered a smile on her face and carried on with the celebration.

Except Luca noticed her anguish.

'Time for bed…' he announced, and there was an endless round of kissing and goodnights so that rather than being nervous of being led to his bedroom, by the time they got there she was actually relieved.

Relieved when he closed the door and it was just the two of them.

'What's going on, Emma?' He meant it this time, wasn't going to be fobbed off again, only she couldn't tell him, just couldn't go there with Luca—not with a man who didn't really want to get involved with her.

And then her phone rang

'Happy birthday, darling!'

'Dad?' She couldn't believe it—she had rung the home before dinner just to say goodnight and had been told that he was resting. Not for a minute had she expected him to remember it was her birthday. 'I couldn't sleep, Em. They let

me come to the nurse's office and ring you...'
Not once growing up had he made a fuss of her.
Everything had been dismissed with words like,
'Oh, you're just like your mother,' and only now
was she starting to get it, only now did she
understand that maybe he had been terrified of
losing her too.

'I love you, baby girl.' And those stars flickered
brighter then as she recalled words used by him
before her mother had gone, the love for her that
had always been there in him but which had taken
illness to help it re-emerge. 'Happy birthday.'

'That was Dad.' She tried to make light of it to
Luca. 'Heaven knows what the nursing home
will charge for a mobile call to Italy...'

He frowned at her pale face. 'Worth it, though?'

'Yes.' She sat on the edge of the bed for a
moment, and then put her head in her hands.

'I found something out,' Emma finally
admitted. 'About her.'

'Your mother?' And she couldn't speak. Tears
that she had always, always pushed back were

trickling down her cheeks. 'I always thought that she'd been living at home when she died, that she didn't want to leave us.'

He knew better than to ask a question now.

'Dad said something last night, and I asked my brother about it. It shouldn't really matter…' She attempted Rory's dismissive take, only it didn't work. 'She walked out on us—a month before the accident. She'd gone to *find herself*, apparently!' Her eyes turned to him for answers. 'I don't know how to feel any more—I don't know who she was. She walked *out* on us….'

'Emma, you can still mourn her, still love her. Who knows what would have happened had she lived? She could have come back, or come to get you…'

Oh, what was the point explaining it to him? Instead, she headed for the bathroom, brushed her teeth and slipped on her candy-striped pyjamas, and when she came out of the bedroom she looked so young, so vulnerable and just so lovely that for Luca there was no question.

Sex *was* off the agenda.

She was just too raw, too vulnerable right now. He did have some moral guidelines and to have her fall in love with him, only for him to then break it off, well, he didn't think he could do it to her.

He lay on his back, staring up at the ceiling, as she climbed into bed beside him.

Every laugh, every word, every chink of glass had him on edge—hell, he hated this house at night.

What did she have to be a virgin for?

He wanted to lose himself in sex, wanted to block everything out except the smell and feel and taste of her. He could hear her crying quietly beside him; he hated tears more than anything, resisted tenderness at all costs, and yet there was no avoiding her tears, nowhere to escape to tonight.

'Emma.' He spoke gently into the darkness. 'Do you want to talk?'

'No!' She was sick of talking, of thinking, and now she had started she couldn't stop crying.

God, he was used to women's tears, but usually when he was ending an affair. He chose women carefully. Yes, Emma had been a gamble, yes, he was attracted to her—to her fiery independence, to the humour, to the fire—and yet she lay beside him, suddenly fragile, and it unnerved him.

He put a hand on her shoulder—was that what he should do? He sort of patted it and she even managed a small smile at his strange attempt at comfort, realising he was exquisitely uncomfortable with her display of emotion.

So was she usually—yet tonight it came in waves, waves that had been building for nearly twenty years.

That first day of school when all the mums had stood at the gates and she had walked in with her brothers.

Her first period, when it had been the school nurse that had explained this terrible thing that had happened and had told her too late that it was all completely normal.

Her first bra, she'd shoplifted it. Long-buried

memories were hurtling in, the one time in her life she'd stolen, but rather that than ask her father to buy one for her.

But always, in her heart, Emma had carried the memory of her mother, sure, quite, quite sure that her mother would have given anything to be there with her.

Only she hadn't, because she'd left her.

And now, lying in bed, she felt as if she was falling.

Anger for all the things she had missed out on was seething inside her.

And she lay in a strange country in a strange bed, with a playboy who didn't deal in emotions when hers were exquisitely raw.

She actually felt sorry for him.

His hand was still patting her in a sort of there, there motion, this slight note of horror in his voice as he felt her shiver at the prospect of the grief she must hold in for now. Yet it was leaking from her eyes, from her breath, this scream inside that was building, the tension in her muscles where she wanted to just run…to curl up, to howl and to weep.

He turned her over to face him.

'Emma, stop this!'

'I can't!' It was like a panic attack, as if she was choking, tears shuddering inside her.

She was this contrary bundle in his arms, tense then pliant, sobbing but distant. He felt her push him away and then he felt her head on his chest, felt the dampness of tears then her furious withdrawal as she wrestled away. And he let her go but she came back and so he comforted her in the only way he knew how—he kissed her.

It infuriated her that this was his answer, enraged her so she almost pushed him out of bed and then wriggled away, appalled. Except it had helped. His mouth, his tongue had flicked her thoughts from pain to pleasure and then he'd stopped.

'I'm sorry,' he whispered.

But Emma wasn't—the room was suddenly too small, the bed too small when her emotions were so big, and she couldn't think, she just couldn't stand to think, so she kissed him back hard. Pressed her red, angry face to his and kissed his mouth fiercely, forcing his lips apart with her tongue, because if he was so good, if this was where it was leading, then better it was now, better this playboy, right?

'Hey.' He pulled down her hands, that were clamped behind his head, and moved his head back.

'Worried you're being used?' Emma jeered.

'I'm not worried about me...' He held her hands and stared into her eyes, and at that second he recognised himself, those nights when he climbed into a woman rather than explore his thoughts—that need for escape, for release. He had just never expected to see it in her—but it was there, and you had to know it to recognise it. 'I'm worried you don't know what you're doing.'

'I want this, Luca.' Oh, yes, she did, she wanted comfort, she wanted *him*!

'I don't want you regretting it…'

'I won't.' She held his eyes and made her promise. 'I won't regret it, Luca. I want this.'

And she did.

She wanted comfort and hell, she was twenty-five! Some time in the future, some time never, when she'd got over him, she could step out into the world of men knowing what it was like to make love with someone.

She wanted to know that so much.

And she wanted him.

All of him.

There was a fuzzy logic in her mind—she was going to lose him anyway so she wanted all of him now. She just had to hold onto her heart, that was all.

'I want this,' she repeated. Of that she was certain. 'I know it's not going anywhere, I know that's not what you want from me…'

Luca stared down at her flushed face and glittering eyes and suddenly he wanted this too.

'One moment.' He stood to go to the bathroom,

his condoms deliberately still unpacked in his toiletry bag, but she caught his arm.

'I'm on the Pill.'

He cursed in Italian. 'Emma...' Her naivety worried him. 'It's not just for pregnancy. You have to make sure he...' It made him wince to think that there would ever be someone else making love to Emma, that he was somehow breaking her in for others to enjoy.

'Do you?' Only she wasn't being naïve, she was bold. 'Always wear one?'

'Always.' Luca swallowed, understanding her meaning—he knew he was healthy and he knew she was too. She was offering him the golden key, yet he hesitated, this rare intimacy alien to him.

It was a tentative kiss, both holding onto their hearts, both refusing for a moment to melt into the sheer, utter bliss of each other.

'We can get rid of these.' Awkward for the first time in the bedroom, he unbuttoned her pyjama top and slid it over her shoulders, removing his own underwear and then sliding off her pyjama bottoms.

The sight of him naked did nothing to still her nerves. She had nothing with which to compare it, except the sealed section of a magazine, but she knew he was pretty spectacular.

'Should we put a towel down or something?' Emma asked, and Luca felt as clinical as a surgeon setting up to operate.

'I'm scared,' Emma admitted. 'Nice scared, but…'

'Me too.' Luca grinned, staring down at his unusually less than responsive manhood, and then he laughed, because it was strange to be talking about *it*, sex, something that usually just, um, happened, and he realised that this had to be better than good—for her sake.

He turned to face her with a strange weight of responsibility on his shoulders, because he wanted this to be right for her. That last kiss had been awkward so he ran his finger along her cheek and then down her arm, and then he stared at the full breasts that had always entranced him, naked now for him to kiss. His hand cupped her lovely bottom and she could feel the wet warmth of his mouth, the tender suckling on her nipples, which made her stomach tighten, and it was a curious warm feeling as his mouth took her breast deeper. And she touched him, too—in awe of his unfurling length against her thigh. Nervous, curious, but brave, she reached down and touched him and Luca closed his eyes at her tender ministrations.

'Is this right?'

He couldn't speak so he nodded and he still couldn't speak so he kissed her instead, not awkwardly this time, and this not a kiss like any he had known—this a tender, slow kiss that led to much more. His hand slid around the front from her bottom, to her most intimate place, where she was moist and warm. He stroked her there until he could hear her slight involuntary whimpers, and then slipped his fingers inside, stretching her slowly, sliding in and out till she was moaning in his arms.

For Emma it was heaven, everything she'd hoped for and nothing like she'd read about—no pain, just bliss, his hand working magic, his mouth back on her nipples now, and she could feel the scratch of hair on his thighs as he moved closer between her legs…

Suddenly there was a need for more contact and he read her thoughts because he pushed her with his body onto her back and he kissed her, not just with his mouth but with his skin, all of him pinning her to the bed, and for a while just the delicious, solid weight of him had her in ecstasy. Then he moved up on his elbows, her legs parting to accommodate him, and he was there at her entrance. She wasn't scared any more, just ready.

She had never been more ready for something in her life.

He was staring down at her with surprising tenderness in his eyes, a gentleness that she had never seen. And she felt as if they were starting something, as if they were going somewhere together. It wasn't just her body she had never trusted to another, but her mind too—and in that moment she let him in, she could feel the first slow, shallow thrusts, feel the stretch of her body as it tried to accommodate him, and the barrier of resistance, and she told herself over and over that she had to remember not to love him.

It hurt, this searing, this moment, and then it was gone—and whatever it was she had just lost, she had found so much more.

The feel of him inside her, the wonders of her own body, rising to greet him as he entered and then resisting each withdrawal—her hips moving to meet his. There was this pull in her stomach, little licks of heat in her thighs. She couldn't keep her eyes open, she was lost in the dark with him and she felt as if she'd been found.

He was moving harder now, and yet she could feel him hold back, only he didn't need to now. Her fingers ran down the length of his back, holding his buttocks and pressing him into her, and Luca had never been closer to anyone, had never been closer to himself, than he was at this moment. She was crying and he was kissing her, demanding, seeking and taking her all. He licked her tears and felt the coil of her legs tighten around him as she gave her urgent consent. He drove in, feeling her in a way he had never felt a woman, the delicious slippery grip of her, the first flickers of her orgasm beating like the first heavy raindrops of a gathering storm. He could feel her mouth on his chest, muffling the pleasure she felt, and he felt her moans vibrate through his heart. Suddenly she was climaxing and so now could he, spilling inside her as she swelled in rhythmic spasms tighter and tighter, dragging him deeper inside her.

He wanted them in this place for ever, could feel his body winding down from the giddy rush, hear his own ragged breathing that heralded the end. Then he did something else he never had before—sated, replete and utterly spent, he looked down at where she lay beneath him and he lowered his head and kissed her.

CHAPTER NINE

EMMA didn't know how she felt when she awoke alone in his bed early the next morning.

The house was already awake, she could hear several voices and the sound of activity as the day before the wedding dawned. In a little while she would join them, would shower and go down and play the part of Luca's girlfriend and help with the preparations in any way that she could, but not just yet.

Now she lay, naked under the sheet, her body tender from last night and her mind surprisingly calm—remembering from a calm distance almost, accepting now what she had always known.

That there could be no going back.

That having made love with Luca, the countdown to the end had started.

She had seen it so many times—with her father, with her brothers, and with Luca himself.

The thrill of the chase, the high on capture, the intense passion of a new relationship—and then, always then, the retreat.

She knew this, had accepted this, had factored it in coolly when she had delivered her demands, but there was one thing she hadn't counted on. As he walked into the bedroom, carrying a laden tray and smiling into her eyes, there was an emotion almost like fear in the eyes that smiled back at him, because she had never anticipated the full effect of him—the dazzling beam of Luca when the full power of his smile, his mind, his body was aimed in her direction.

He'd be hell to miss.

He was dressed in jeans and nothing else. Barefoot and bare chested, he walked across the bedroom towards her, and it was a Luca she had never seen.

Usually suited, clean shaven—even the times

she had seen him dressed rather more casually, still there had been a formal air to him. But it was a different Luca in front of her now.

Unshaven, his hair damp from the shower, it flopped forward as he bent over her. Then he took the coffee pot from the tray and put it on the bedside table before placing a tray on her lap. He looked younger somehow, less austere perhaps, and for Emma terribly, dangerously, devastatingly beautiful.

'It is chaos out there.' His thumb gestured to the bedroom door. 'So we will hide in here for a couple of hours.'

'Shouldn't I be out there, helping?' Emma asked, reaching for the pot of coffee, but Luca got there first.

'I'll pour,' Luca said, then answered her question. 'No, as I just said to my mother, we would only get in the way.'

Only she wasn't really listening—instead, she stared at the cup he filled. It had been a seemingly innocuous gesture, yet for Emma it was huge.

He'd brought her breakfast in bed.

Oh, she'd had staff knock on the door of her hotel room at six a.m. when she was travelling with Luca and bring her in her order, but never, not once in her life, had someone who wasn't being paid prepared breakfast for her, brought it to her and expected her to just sit as they poured. Always she got up, always it was her...

And this morning it was *him*.

It was scary how nice it felt to be looked after, even in this small way.

'These are *pizelles*. Like waffles...' He smeared one with honey and handed it to her—and then lay on his side, propped up on one arm, his coffee in the other hand, watching her intently, scanning her features for remorse.

'How are you?' he finally asked outright.

'Good,' Emma said through a mouthful of *pizelle*.

'Any regrets?' he asked.

'None,' she shook her head. 'You?'

'None—so long as you're okay?' he pressed.

'The first time's supposed to be awful,' she murmured a little wickedly.

'Says who?' he asked, outraged.

'I read it in a magazine.'

Luca rolled his eyes.

'If that was awful…' Emma giggled '…I can't wait for bad!'

'Throw away the magazines, baby…' He took her coffee cup and her *pizelle* away and straddled her on the bed. 'I'll teach you everything I know.'

It was such a different Luca, as if she'd been looking at him through the wrong end of a telescope. His energy was lighter, funnier, sexier even, if that were possible. They shared breakfast and then each other, and then they left the chaotic household and had a picnic on the beach.

This time she didn't slip away when it was time to ring her father, she just sat on the blanket and laughed and listened to him reminiscing, and it was so much easier with Luca lying there beside her.

'I'll sort out the back fees for the home,' Luca said as she clicked off the phone. She turned to him, appalled.

'How did you know?'

'I read the letter the nursing home gave you,' he admitted shamelessly.

'That's reprehensible!' She was furious, embarrassed... And then he kissed her.

'Sorted,' Luca said, and he caught her eyes, 'You've helped me—now I can help you. I absolutely insist on it.'

And it was probably no big deal to him, except for Emma it was.

She felt the lightness as six months of worry slipped away, felt the elation as they ran down to the beach and enjoyed the late afternoon, felt the joy of being a couple, having someone to lean on, helping each other out.

And then Emma did a stupid thing.

As he kissed her in the salty sea, as she felt the waves rush round them and the chase of his tongue in her mouth, she started to wonder.

Started to hope.

Their day at the beach had brought a glow to her skin and on the morning of the wedding Emma massaged in body oil, glad of the peace in their bedroom and the chance, for once, to take her time getting ready, without Luca snapping his fingers and telling her she looked fine as she was.

Most of the house had been commandeered by the bride and her entourage. The whir of the hair-dryer had been continual from eight a.m. and there was a constant stream of flowers, including the traditional arrival of flowers for the bride from the groom, which Emma was summoned down in her dressing gown to witness. As Rico was conserving his depleted energy for the wedding, Luca had stepped into father-of-the-bride duty and Emma had a little giggle to herself to see the usually unruffled Luca, who could handle the most difficult client or tense boardroom meeting with ease, just a touch frazzled as he dealt not just with his sister's theatrics but vases and flowers and the hairdresser, who was trying to locate a free power point for heated rollers.

Yes, their bedroom was a nice place to be!

Because she could, Emma spent time on her

hair, attempting what a hairdresser had once, when she'd been to her brother Rory's wedding—taking several curls at a time and wrapping them around her wand till it fell in one thick heavy ringlet. Over and over she did this and for once her hair behaved, for once Emma was pleased with the results.

The hot September weather meant foundation wouldn't see the service out, so she put just a slip of silver eye shadow on her lids, relying mainly on lashings of mascara, a quick sweep of pink on her cheeks and a shimmer of tinted lip gloss. In her dash to shop and get ready for the trip, Emma had relied heavily on the stylist's suggestion of a suitable dress, although Emma hadn't been at all sure that it was right for a wedding when she'd tried it on in the boutique.

The silver-grey dress had looked very plain, if a touch short, in the shop, but the assistant had assured her it would look marvellous with the right shoes and make-up.

It did.

It slipped over her head, the material shimmering more in the natural light and the superb cut of the delicate fabric turned her most loathed bits into voluptuous curves.

Staring at her reflection in the mirror, Emma was slightly taken aback by what she saw. It was as if she'd grown up in these few days—gone from young lady to woman, and Emma knew it had little to do with her birthday and a lot more to do with the man who was now walking into the bedroom.

'I must get changed…' His voice trailed off as she turned to face him—and he suddenly felt that walking into his room to find her there was like coming across a haven of tranquility in a madhouse.

He'd appreciated her all morning—so many of his girlfriends would have been demanding their hour with the hairdresser while simultaneously demanding yet more of his time, yet Emma had left him to deal with his family—no sulking, or pouting, just that lovely smile when she'd briefly come down, and now he'd walked into the bedroom to this. Oh, he'd seen her dressed formally on many occasions, only this was different—a wedding, a family affair, his Luca plus one.

His diamonds on her ears were as sparkling as her eyes and there was that glimpse again, that small glimpse of how life could be for him if he hadn't made the choices that he had.

Of a life he could have with her.

'We leave in ten minutes,' he said, his voice gruff with suppressed emotion. He'd already showered and shaved, so he quickly pulled off his casual shirt and trousers and dressed in the dark wedding suit and gunmetal grey tie that had been chosen for the men of the wedding party, or rather that Emma had chosen for them. He had refused, point blank, to consider the burgundy monstrosities his sister had insisted would match the bridesmaids, and Emma had found the perfect one.

Not *the one*, but the *perfect* one.

Making a rare effort, he combed some sculpting gel through his thick hair then splashed on cologne. He filled his pockets with various envelopes for the priest and the band and then, when his head was around it, when more rational thought had descended, he spoke.

'You look lovely.'

'Thank you.' She gave a brief smile at his clipped tone, insecure enough to worry that he privately thought she looked awful.

'I will be busy today, back and forth with relatives. With my father ill, that duty…'

'It's no problem.' Emma smiled, putting some tissues in her bag and then squirting her perfume—just as she always did last thing before they went out. It was *these* little things he was noticing, Luca realised, these small details that added up to Emma. Her perfume was reaching him and her entire being was too.

Today was a day he had been dreading for months, since the wedding date had been announced and the preparations had begun. It had hung over him like a black cloud—being with his family, *all* his family, smiling and joking and keeping up the pretence, the charade, that there was no rotten core to the D'Amatos—yet here in this room he could breathe.

He couldn't not kiss her.

He lowered his head and his lips gently found hers, just pressing a little into the luscious flesh of her mouth, and he felt a flutter of something sweet and good and right settle.

Only their lips met, gently touching, barely moving, just tiny pulse-like kisses as they breathed each other's air, and it was a kiss like no other, this rare, weary tenderness from Luca that made her feel beautiful and wanted and somehow sad too.

'This is so much better with you here.'

There was a sting at the back of her throat and she couldn't understand why something so nice should make her feel like crying.

'It could always be.' She'd crossed the line, she knew she had. She'd taken the present and hinted at a future—there was suddenly no breath on her cheek as Luca stilled, no acknowledgment as to what she had said, but it circled in the air between them.

'We must go.' He waited at the bedroom door as with shaking hands she reapplied her lip gloss, catching her eyes in the mirror and giving herself a stern reminder of the terms that she had agreed to.

It was the most gorgeous, moving wedding.

Even if she couldn't understand much of what was said, even if she was here under false pretences and was supposed to be playing a part, the tears that filled her eyes weren't manufactured as the proud, frail father of the bride walked his glowing daughter down the aisle.

There were only two dry eyes in the church and they both belonged to Luca.

He stood, taller than the rest, his back ramrod straight, and though he did all the right things, there was a remoteness to him—an irritable edge that Emma couldn't quite define, an impatience perhaps for the service to be over. For the second it was, the first moment that he could, she felt his hand tighten around hers as he led her swiftly outside.

'These two will be next!' Mia teased, holding her husband's hand, laughing and chatting with her relatives.

'When?' Rico's eyes met his son's.

'Leave it, Pa,' Luca said, but Rico could not.

'What about the D'Amato name?' he pressed.

'Soon, Rico!' Mia soothed. 'I'm sure it will happen soon.'

There was an exquisitely uncomfortable moment, because it was clear soon was far too long for Rico, but his brother Rinaldo lightened things. 'They leave things much longer now.' He squeezed his young wife's waist. 'Not like me…' He kissed her heavily made-up cheek then murmured, 'I wasn't going to let you slip away.'

As Rico greeted other guests and Rinaldo and his wife drifted off, Mia chided Luca for his stern expression, talking in Italian then giving a brief translation for Emma.

'Luca was close to Zia Maria, Rinaldo's first wife,' she explained to Emma, then looked over at Luca. 'You cannot expect him to be on his own.'

'He didn't even wait a year,' Luca retorted, his voice ice-cold on this warm day.

'Luca—not here,' Mia pleaded, then turned to Emma. 'Come, let me introduce you to my sister.'

Emma lost Luca along the way, chatting to aunts, congratulating Daniela—really, she was doing well. Through her work she knew enough about Luca to answer the most difficult questions, though it would have been far easier if he was by her side.

They were starting to call relatives for more photos now and she found him behind the church, walking between the tombstones, standing and pausing, his shoulders rigid, almost as if he were at a funeral rather than a wedding.

'You're wanted for the photos,' she said softly,

her eyes following his gaze to the tombstone he was reading.

'My grandmother,' Luca explained.

'She was so young,' Emma said, reading the inscription. His grandmother had been little older than her mother when she'd died.

'I don't remember her really—a little perhaps.' He shrugged as if it didn't matter, but clearly from his grim expression it did. 'And this is Zia Maria. I *do* remember her…'

Emma licked dry lips as she saw the young age of his aunt too. 'Rinaldo's first wife…'

'She was a lovely woman.' His voice was tender in memory, and pensive too.

'I know what you meant about Rinaldo…' He closed his eyes on her as if she couldn't possibly know, but Emma did. 'About not even waiting a year to remarry. I hated how many girlfriends my dad had. I know now that Mum had left him and everything, but he started dating so soon after…'

Now that she knew, it was as if her brain was

finally allowing her to remember—patchy, hazy memories that she couldn't really see but could *feel*—a woman who wasn't her mother kissing her father, women's *things* in the bathroom, the sound of female laughter drifting across the landing to her bedroom as she lay weeping into the pillow and wanting her mother.

'They make me sick!' He shook his head, then raked his hair back in a gesture of tense frustration. 'Just leave it.'

And she had no choice but to do that, because now really wasn't the time. 'We should get back anyway.' She turned to go, but he was still staring at his aunt's grave and Emma guessed he must be painfully aware that in a matter of days or weeks he would be back here in the graveyard to bury his father. Only she didn't understand what he was doing here today, when everyone was trying to be happy, reminding himself when he should be forgetting.

'Luca…'

'You go. I'll be there soon.'

'Luca, today is a wedding—your family are waiting for the photos. For now, surely you should try to forget?' she said hesitantly.

'I never forget.' It was a bald statement and his eyes met hers for the first time since she had joined him in the cemetery, but there was none of the warmth that had been there that morning. In fact, there was no warmth at all. 'Come—we have a job to do.'

And in that short sentence he both reminded and relegated her. This was just a weekend away to him, a deal that had been struck, a pact that had been reached—an act she had agreed to partake in. It was Emma who had forgotten that at times; Luca clearly always remembered it.

As they joined the rest of his family, as they stood side by side with her hand in his, never had it been harder for her to force a smile.

CHAPTER TEN

IT HAD been a long exhausting day and was a long exhausting evening—as weddings often are.

Rico made it through dinner and, as Mia watched on anxiously, he managed to dance with his daughter. After that, clearly unable to participate further, Rico took a back seat and it was for Luca to take up the baton.

There was nothing Emma could put her finger on as Luca took over the role of patriarch with ease. He chatted with everyone, sat with the men at a table for a while and she could see him laughing at jokes, raising his glass in a toast, joining in tapping spoons to demand that the newlyweds kiss—and when she came over, he was soundly slapped on the back for his choice in women.

'The D'Amato name goes on,' Uncle Rinaldo cheered, so clearly she would do! 'Salute!'

There was just something…

Something that filled the air between them as they waved off the bride and groom.

As they put his parents into a car and then stayed to say farewell to the last of the guests.

Something as he let them into the darkened house. He climbed into the bed beside her and stared unseeingly into the darkness.

A shout from the house snapped Emma's eyes open, her body instinctively moving to investigate, but he caught her wrist.

'It is just Pa, calling for his pain medication.'

His fingers were loose, but there. That small contact became her sole focus, every nerve darting along its pathways to locate and gather where his fingers touched hers.

She listened to the sound of silence and thought how hard it must be, not just for Rico but for Mia with the exhausting, round-the-clock care she delivered. And Luca must be thinking it too, for she could feel him—the tense energy in the room, this state of hyper-vigilance this family must live with when dealing with someone so ill.

Had it been like this for him as a child too?

She had never known violence—oh, there had been arguments and, living with four men, yes, the occasional fight, but they had been storms that had blown over quickly. This was different. A thick tension had slowly built as they lay there together—yet he would have lain here alone as a child, and heard every creak, every bang, every word while wondering if…

'Luca?' She knew he was awake even if he was ignoring her. 'How bad was it?'

'Leave it, Emma.'

'You can tell me.'

'I don't want to.'

And it should have ended it. She expected him to turn away, except he didn't. Instead, he turned on his side, towards her. 'Emma, please…' He didn't finish what he was saying, or had he just said it? This begging for distraction.

He moved his body over hers, and then his lips were on hers, his kiss catching her by complete surprise. Luca's mouth was seeking an urgent distraction; it was a frenetic, heated kiss that urged her body into instant response. They had made love over and over, Luca initiating her into the wonders of her body, the marvel of his, only this was nothing like the tender, slow love-making of previous times—this an enthralling new facet. Urgency crashed in like a stormy ocean slamming onto the beach, and her body flared in instant response to his potent maleness. He was kissing her, hot, demanding kisses that she reciprocated, her fingers at the back of his head pressing his face closer to hers. His thighs came down hard on hers, his arms swept under her, circling her, craving more contact—as too did she.

She opened her centre to him, parting her legs, yearning for that first thrust of him with the hunger of an addict. Only it didn't bring relief, the feel of him driving inside her, his skin sliding over her, it just made her want more, energy building like a cyclone, swirling and obliterating and dragging her to its centre. He moved his arms from beneath her and there was the sensation of falling as her back hit the mattress and Luca leant in on his elbows. Over and over he kissed her, over and over he said her name into the air as he gulped it in, into her mouth as he licked her.

Her orgasms had, till now, been slowly coaxed from her, a learned thing, this gradual build-up as he taught her to let go, as he urged her on to lose her mind, herself, to new sensations. But this night in his bed she was swept into a maelstrom of sensation that was as desperate and urgent as Luca's fierce need.

The shudder of him inside her was met with sweet beats of her own—it wasn't scx, it was devotion, the intensity of her orgasm startling her. Her hips moved frantically upwards to escape from the relentless throb of her body, but Luca was in instant pursuit, his last throes tipping her to a place there could be no coming back from, to true abandon, to utter trust.

They slept together—the third night in his bed, and this time they truly slept together, coiled around each other in a fierce embrace that didn't abate with sleep.

Never did he just glance at his mother in the morning.

Never could he just accept that greeting and coffee without thought.

Always he checked.

And all these years later, still it happened— an instant check that, for Luca, was as natural as breathing.

A cardigan on a hot summer's morning.

Or the unusual sight of her in full make-up at seven a.m.

Or worse, an empty kitchen and the explanation of a migraine as to why she couldn't get up.

His dark eyes automatically scanned for clues or confirmation, yearning for that same rush of momentary relief he had sometimes felt as a child, that all was well—for today at least. That surely his father was too old, too sick, too frail to hurt her... Ah, but he had a savage tongue too—and words, if they were savage enough, could sometimes hurt as much as a blow.

'How was he last night?' Luca asked in his native language, watching his mother stiffen.

'It went wonderfully,' she replied evasively.

'I meant how were things when you got home? How was Pa?'

'Tired,' Mia said briefly. 'Where is Emma?'

'Still asleep.' Climbing out of that bed, feeling her stir, he had hushed her and kissed her back to sleep and then stood and watched her sleeping. Young, innocent, trusting—how could he do it to her? How could he take her by the hand and lead her to hell? He felt as if his home was built on a sewer—he could almost smell the filth beneath the very foundations as he sat at the table and his mother embroidered the lies.

'He did so well to dance with Daniela...Leo is

coming this morning and his nurse Rosa. I am a bit worried, because he coughed all night—it was a very long day for him.'

'For you too,' Luca pointed out, and then added, 'I heard him shout in the night.'

'He just shouts, Luca, nothing else…' Mia closed her eyes. 'He is old and weak and tired…'

'Yet still he treats you poorly.'

'Words don't hurt me, Luca,' Mia said. 'Please just leave things alone—it is good that you came.'

The coffee tasted like acid in his mouth—her words rendering him hopeless.

Again.

For everything he had a solution, an answer. His logical, analytical brain could take the most complex problem and unravel it to the base solution. Yet nothing—not logic, not reason, not power, not brawn, not wealth—could solve this.

Nothing!

'Leave him.' He stood up, stared into her eyes and even as he pleaded again, he knew it was futile, as futile now as it always had been.

'You know I cannot!'

'You can…' His usually strong voice cracked, and he saw his mother flinch—both of them re-alising that he was near to tears. It had been so long since he had even been close to crying that the sting in his eyes, the swell in his throat caught even Luca by surprise. The pain, the fear, the helplessness, the never-ending grief he had lived with as a child was still there—right there and ready to return at any given moment—the anguish waiting to floor him. 'Leave, Ma.'

'He is dying, Luca. How can I leave a dying man? What would people think?'

'What does it matter?' Luca burst out.

'It matters!' Mia sobbed. 'And he matters too. He is sick, he is scared…'

'He wasn't always sick! He can be moved to hospital.'

'Luca. Please. I beg you to stop this.'

She didn't want his help—she simply didn't want it, yet he could not accept that.

'He is a bastard, and he has always been a

bastard,' Luca tried again. 'That he is dying does not change that fact.'

'He's my husband.'

Those three little words that had condemned her to a lifetime of pain and suffering.

The shame of leaving, the scandal attached to such an action had silenced her and in turn had silenced Luca too.

It hadn't always silenced him.

He had spat in his father's face many times as a child—and he still bore the scars to prove it.

He had tried to intervene when he was twelve years old, and had been beaten to within an inch of his life for his trouble.

And always Mia had sobbed—always she had pleaded that he ignore what his father was doing, that he was making things worse.

So he had waited.

Waited for his moment, waited till he was taller, fitter, stronger—and then one night, when the inevitable had happened, an eighteen-year-old boy in the body of a man had intervened.

Eighteen years of tension and frustration, combined with a generous dash of testosterone, had exploded, and he had beaten and bullied his father that night as mercilessly as his father had beaten and bullied his mother over the years—sure this would end it, sure that finally it was over.

Yet the next morning, his knuckles bruised and bleeding, his top lip swollen, his left eye closed, his cheek a savage mess, something inside Luca had crumbled and died when his mother had walked into the kitchen—bruises that hadn't been there last night on her face, her arms a pitiful mass of red and blue. But worse than that had been the accusing look in her eyes as she'd faced her son, telling him that he had made things even worse, that his interference hadn't helped. And then she had said the words that would stay with Luca for ever.

'*Siete no migliore del vostro padre.*'

'You are no better than your father,' Mia had told him as Luca had sat appalled at what he had done and sick with what she said next. 'It is as I always feared—you are just like him.'

'Don't make things worse, Luca,' his mother said now, and her words dragged him straight through the coals of hell from the past to the even more hellish, hopeless present. 'There is nothing you can do. Having Emma here has made things better.' Mia gave a tired smile. 'He is proud that perhaps his name will continue, and that has appeased him for a while.' Her eyes anxiously scanned Luca's face. 'She is a wonderful girl—I am pleased. It helps in other ways too...' Mia admitted. 'Seeing that you are finally happy. But please look after her, Luca, and don't let your past...' Her voice strangled off into silence, and Luca shut his eyes. 'Soon, one day, there are things I must tell you—about your past, your history...' she finally managed to add.

But he knew them all already, had worked it out long ago.

Vigilance and tombstones had taught him the unenviable truth.

And now, on this morning, discovering that his mother thought he might be capable of the violence of his father, that his mother, who loved him, worried for the woman who was starting to— That the most innocent of them all slept upstairs in his bed, was, for Luca, an added torment.

'There are things you need to know, things we have to face,' Mia said.

Not if Luca could avoid them.

Rinaldo's words rang in his ears. *'The D'Amato name goes on. Salute!'*

Not if Luca could help it.

The last D'Amato—he was it. He had sworn that on his Aunt Maria's grave, that night when he'd been eighteen. He had sworn that the D'Amato line ended with him.

If he could keep his heart closed, never fall in love, then he could never cause pain to anyone else.

It really was that simple.

CHAPTER ELEVEN

EMMA DRESSED in khaki shorts and a white halter-neck top and sandals and applied some light make-up, but gave up on her hair—if she brushed out the serum and lacquer, it would end up all fluffy, so instead she ran her fingers through it and tied it in a low ponytail, then tentatively made her way down to the kitchen.

'Good morning.' Luca stood and kissed her, but didn't meet her eyes. Instead, he introduced her to a rather formidable man who was sitting at the table. 'This is Leo, Dr Calista—he was called out yesterday to an emergency, so he could not make the wedding. And this is Rosa, the nurse.'

Rosa was at the kitchen bench, measuring out medication, and gave Emma a brief smile, then turned her attention back to her work. Dr Leo Calista was more formal than the people she had met so far. Instead of kissing her on the cheeks, as everyone else had, he stood as she entered and shook Emma's hand. He was also familiar to her and Emma frowned as she tried to place him.

'I was in the UK for a conference recently!' He smiled at her confusion. 'I dropped in to see Luca to update him on his father...'

'No, that's not how I know you.' Emma frowned, sure that she would remember.

'We have spoken on the phone.'

And that must be it. 'It's nice to meet you.'

'You too. And as a near local now! It is good to see Luca bring a friend here; you are welcome.'

'Thank you,' she replied, a little bewildered.

'Gradite unirli per la prima colazione?' Mia offered, inviting the doctor to join the family for breakfast, but Dr Calista declined, instead asking if he might see Rico.

'He seems nice,' Emma observed as the trio made their way out of the kitchen.

'He's a good doctor. He is from the village, he studied medicine in Roma, then returned, but always he keeps up to date. He has been good to my family,' Luca explained. 'His care has meant my father can be looked after at home.'

'That must mean a lot.'

'It does to my mother, but I think that my father should be in hospital—now that the wedding is over. I spoke with Leo before…'

'What did he say?' Emma asked.

'That it is not my choice. That my father wants to die at home and my mother wants to nurse him.'

'Then you have to respect their wishes…' Her voice trailed off as she saw his sharp expression, and there was a pause, a long tense pause as Luca made the decision, as he picked the fight…

And let her go.

'Don't tell me how to deal with my family, Emma—you can drop the concerned act when there is no one else present.'

'Act?' She had missed the change—was still

working on yesterday's clock. Yesterday, when he had held her, kissed her, adored her, and it took a moment to flick to the new time zone Luca now demanded she adjust to.

'When we let people think we are together.'

'There was no one present in the bedroom last night,' Emma pointed out, 'but that didn't stop you making love to me.'

'Making love?' Wide eyes mocked her, a cruel smile on his face as he jeered, 'Why do women always call it that?'

God, but he could be sadistic. She could feel tears sting her eyes but she refused to let them fall. 'Because that's how it felt at the time, Luca.'

'It was just sex, that's what I'm paying you for, Emma, if you remember rightly. Remind me again, how much are the back fees for your father's home?' And then he was silenced, her hand slicing the air to meet his cheek, but his hand caught her wrist before it made contact.

'That would be extremely silly.'

'You're utterly despicable!' she gasped.

'Brilliant in bed, though. Tell me again, how much are the back fees for your father?' Luca drawled. 'Pillow talk is just that, Emma, you said yourself it is what men do.'

'This wasn't about *money*,' she denied, because his offer to help her had come after she'd slept with him. God, she hated him, hated what he was doing to her and that she didn't understand why he was doing it.

'I hate you!' she cried.

'Good,' Luca said calmly. 'Good—hate me, loathe me. Better that than love me, because I will not love you back, Emma. I told you that from the start. I made it exceptionally clear. Don't go getting teary now and complaining, just because the sex is too good.'

There was nothing she could say to that, nothing because the door was opening and he dropped her wrist as Dr Calista walked in. Clearly sensing the thick atmosphere, he asked in English if there was a problem.

Emma didn't answer, appalled by Luca's

words but more appalled by her action—if he hadn't halted her she would have hit him. She held her wrist where he had stopped her, his words still stinging as the doctor asked his question again.

'Is everything okay?'

'Yes.' Emma's voice gathered strength. 'Everything's fine.'

'Actually, it isn't,' Luca snapped. 'My mother is exhausted. How much longer must she nurse him at home before you admit him?'

'Luca, I am trying to respect your parents' wishes.'

'Which means you are only respecting my father's wishes.' Luca's lip curled as he added, 'That is all my mother does.' He turned to Emma. 'Can you excuse us, please?'

As she left the room they faced each other, two proud, impressive men.

'I am not leaving till my father is admitted to hospital,' Luca said.

'Then you may be here for a while, Luca.'

Leo's words were born of exasperation. 'Luca, what is going on?'

'Nothing.' He was eighteen years old again, Leo slicing the needle through the raw flesh of his cheek and asking questions, Luca pretending that he had a hangover, that there had been a fight in the next village...

'I'm worried about you, Luca.'

'Worry about my mother.'

'That I do,' Leo said, 'and Emma too.'

'Emma?' Luca's voice was incredulous. 'You worry about *Emma*?'

'I heard you fighting, and I could see the bruises on her wrist. I know this is a tense time,' the doctor said, and Luca opened his mouth to make excuses, to lie, to cover up, to hide from it, except he didn't. It was like a fist in his stomach—he had done nothing wrong, logic told him that, he had been stopping Emma from hitting him, that was all—and yet he felt as if he were being handed the baton.

The D'Amato curse being passed onto him,

when he had sworn the line would be finally broken.

Only, unlike his father, Luca faced it.

Stood there and faced the truth.

And knew he had to deal with it.

'I'm staying for a few days.' Luca walked into the bedroom where Emma lay on the bed, staring upwards. He could feel her pain, sense her confusion and he could see the purple marks his fingers had left on her tender skin. He flinched inside but let nothing of his horror show on his face or in his voice. 'You should pack.' Luca's head inclined to the wardrobe. 'I'll arrange the transport and ring Evelyn to cancel my diary for a week—I will stay on for a while. When you're back can you speak with Kasumi…' And he reeled off his orders, spoke of nothing but work and even managed to look her straight in the eyes as he did so.

'I take it that means business as usual?' Emma got his point—oh, she so got the point!

'That was what you wanted. I assured you that you wouldn't lose your job over this. Of course...' he gave a brief, mirthless smile '...if you choose to leave, I will provide an excellent reference. I have some contacts...'

He wanted her gone.

With no excuse or explanation, he just wanted her gone.

'What happened, Luca?' she wanted to know. She just didn't get it. 'Everything was wonderful...'

'For a little while, perhaps,' Luca said. 'But I'm bored with you now.'

'Should I send myself some flowers?' Emma sneered. 'That's what you usually make me do.'

'Buy yourself a leaving gift,' Luca suggested.

'Who said I'm leaving?' She damn well *wouldn't* give him the satisfaction. 'When did I say that I was looking for other work?' Deep beneath the pain of his dismissal, there amidst her loss, there was a small coup—a little surge of triumph as, though his expression appeared unmoved, she registered the slight bob of his Adam's apple and knew she had unnerved him. She felt a little flicker of satisfaction as she refused to dance to his beastly tune. 'I'm very happy where I am—unless you have any complaints about my work?'

She watched his lips tighten just a fraction before he answered.

'None.'

'Good, then I shall see you on your return.' She took off the earrings and attempting some dignity held them out to him, but Luca merely shrugged.

'Consider them a bonus.'

And just like that she was dismissed from his personal life, *they* were dismissed, everything they had shared these past days was cheapened and soiled.

'While we're still on personal time, before it's back to business…' There were no tears in her eyes, no waver in her voice, as she meant every word. 'I hate you.'

'You're repeating yourself now.'

'Just so you know,' Emma said, in a voice that was surprisingly clear. 'When I smile and bring you in your coffee, or laugh at one of your jokes, or join you at some function, or when you think that I've forgotten what you did...' Her eyes briefly met his. 'I haven't. Just so you remember...I hate you.'

CHAPTER TWELVE

S HE *was* preparing to leave.

Quietly, imperceptibly perhaps, but preparing all the same.

Like the lights being switched off in an office block, one by one, she closed the little doors to her heart—applying for other jobs, preparing her art portfolio, being more assertive with the real estate agent—all the while working alongside the man who had shattered her heart.

She had been back at her desk the next morning, ringing his clients, cancelling meetings, chatting with Evelyn, refusing to grant him his undoubted wish and immediately remove herself from his life so that he didn't have to look at his *mistake*.

She'd take small victories where she could find them, and absolutely refused to be rushed.

And when his father was finally admitted to hospital and he returned, it was *more* business than usual.

Efficient, competent, she got on with her work and, on his first day back, she brought him in coffee and offered a pleasant good morning— and very deliberately set the tone.

'Good morning, Luca.'

'Good morning, Emma.'

Had she not known better, Emma might have been fooled for a second into thinking this was hurting him as much as it was her.

He looked awful.

Oh, by any other standards he looked divine, but there was an ashy tinge to his complexion, a fleck of silver in his hair she was sure hadn't been there before, and the neck of his shirt was just a touch too loose, yet it looked as if it was choking him.

'Your client meeting isn't till nine. Evelyn has

asked if I can go through your schedule for the next fortnight, if you've got time.'

She had been practising hard for this moment—Luca knew that. She didn't blush, or avoid his gaze, and there wasn't even a hint of aggression as she spoke. Never had he admired her more.

'Now's fine.' He nodded for her to sit and pulled up his schedule on his computer as Emma took notes.

'You've two international trips scheduled…'

'Three,' Luca said. 'We will need to stay overnight in Paris.'

'I thought…' Her pen was poised over the paper. As Evelyn had started another round of IVF, it meant Emma would be accompanying him on all trips—the prospect was almost more than she could bear. 'I mean with your father being unwell, Evelyn wasn't sure that you still wanted—'

'Paris is closer to Italy than London,' Luca interrupted. 'I won't be cancelling anything—in fact, after taking a week off, there is a lot to catch up on. I'll need one of you to stay back late tonight.'

'Of course,' Emma said evenly.

'Probably tomorrow too.'

Emma knew what he was doing—he was warning her just how difficult this would be if she chose to pursue it, because it was she who would be doing the bulk of the travelling—she was here to lighten Evelyn's load after all.

'Not a problem!' She gave him a smile. 'Was there anything else?'

Leave.

He didn't answer her, but it was the word that thrummed in his head during every meeting, every flight, every overseas trip.

Leave, his mind willed her—because it was killing him to be so close to her and not be able to have her.

He had thought it hard breaking things off with Martha—had thought for years that Martha had been 'the one', quietly safe in the knowledge that it would never be that hard again...

This was a thousand times worse.

Maybe she should just give him his wish, Emma thought over and over in the ensuing weeks as she worked alongside him, refusing to give in—it would certainly be easier to.

But she couldn't quite close that last little door, couldn't just sever all ties—and for one very good reason.

'What star sign would the tenth of June be?' Evelyn had given up trying not to hope—she had a blood test in a couple of days that would determine her fate, and was frantically working out dates.

'Gemini.' Emma smiled, then put her head down and got on with her work.

'What are Geminis like?' Evelyn pushed, and Emma hesitated. She'd seen Evelyn's devastation once and was dreading it happening again, yet was trying not to show it.

'Charming, happy, witty,' Emma said, wishing Evelyn wouldn't get her hopes up so, but, then, who could blame her? It was, of course, all

Evelyn could think about, all that was on her mind, no matter how she tried to get on with her day.

Emma could empathise with that.

'I know I'm going over the top...' Evelyn stood up to join Luca for his two p.m. meeting and glancing over and seeing Emma's worried face, misconstrued it. 'I think sometimes you just know—I feel different this time, I just know that I'm pregnant.'

For Evelyn's sake, Emma prayed she was right.

For her own sake, she was frantically hoping that Evelyn was wrong because she was feeling different too. She pushed the thought firmly out of her mind and forced herself to concentrate on her busy afternoon.

Emma could hardly believe the variations in her workload. One minute she was arranging seven-star hotels in Dubai, the next she was dealing with a hysterical housekeeper on the phone and a dog that was convulsing.

Just another day behind the scenes of Luca D'Amato's busy life.

Evelyn was with him in a meeting, so she texted her rather than rang.

There's a problem with Pepper.

Housekeeper has to leave soon.

Vet on way.

She hit 'send'—knew what the reply would be and wearily picked up her bag and summoned a driver to take her straight to Luca's.

Somehow she hadn't been to his apartment since that day—since their first kiss.

Stepping inside, it was hard to recall her innocence, her naivety—that she had thought that she could handle things, could somehow deal with the force of his charm and his hot-and-cold affection and come out unscathed.

'The vet's coming!' Rita, his housekeeper, was in tears as she bent over the little dog. 'He's just a few minutes away. I have to get to school to pick up the children.'

Pepper was a sad sight, lying on the floor in obvious distress but snapping and snarling if anyone approached.

'You go,' Emma said. 'I'll wait for the vet.'

'Luca will be devastated,' Rita sobbed. 'He loves that little dog.'

'Really?' Emma couldn't keep the note of surprise from her voice. 'He's hardly ever here to see him.'

'But he liked to come home to him,' Rita said, emotion countering discretion. 'Oh, poor Pepper. I could never understand Martha just leaving him behind...'

Emma hated this.

Left alone with Pepper, she *hated* this.

These glimpses into Luca were killing her.

Working with him was bad enough, travelling with him too, but she could almost deal with business, only this job involved his personal life too...

Being in his home—amongst his things—sitting trying to comfort a little snapping, snarling, terrified dog that had belonged to a woman he had once loved, was more than she could take, more than she could bear…

'Where's the damn vet?'

She hadn't been counting on Luca arriving, she had never thought he would dash out of an important meeting for a little dog he didn't seem to particularly like.

'He's two minutes away—he just rang.'

He knelt down beside the little dog, his face grim and his voice not particularly tender.

'You're fine,' he said to Pepper in a gruff voice, and then glanced up at Emma. 'If I start being all nice he'll realise…' He put his hand out to the dog who bared his teeth and Luca ignored it, just stroked the little thing, and Emma watched as finally Pepper relaxed. 'You know you like it really, you know you won't bite me,' Luca said, and then, when the intercom buzzed, he addressed Emma.

'Can you let the vet in on your way out?'

'I don't mind staying.'

'There's no need.'

He was stroking the little dog with both hands now, soothing it and calming it and now saying nice things. She just didn't get him—never, ever would she get him!

'Should you ring Martha?' she asked and watched him freeze for a moment.

'She left him,' he snapped. 'It's not her dog any more.'

'Why did you two break up?' she asked curiously. Now maybe wasn't the right time for this discussion, but it was the only window she had, the only possible time to ask the question she had for so long wondered about.

'Things weren't going too well,' Luca said. 'Here's the vet now—let him in and then go.'

'Or they were going too well?' Emma stood up. 'What, you were too happy, Luca, so you had to break it off with her?'

'Just leave.'

But she couldn't, instead she said what was on her mind. 'Are you worried you might turn out like your dad?' His face was black with anger as he turned to her, except he didn't scare her. 'You're not your father, Luca.'

'Don't practise your high-school psychology on me,' Luca sneered. 'I don't love you, Emma— in fact, I don't actually like you.' His words were very deliberate and aimed straight for her heart. 'I slept with you because you wanted it, because you begged me for it. I warned you from the start an affair was all it could be. Now, when I tell you, as I did from the start, that it would not last, you have to find a *reason* why I ended it.'

'Okay, Luca,' she said, feeling sick, 'I get the message.'

'No, you ask, I answer—the reason I ended it is because, like the rest, you got too clingy, too needy...and frankly—' all his attention was on Pepper now '—you're not that interesting in bed.'

She closed her eyes and swayed on her feet.

'Out,' he said, without turning his head.

This time Emma went.

* * *

It was quick and it was painless and it absolutely had to be done.

Even with a dog-sitter and a housekeeper, there had always been a small dash of guilt at leaving him so much—but as the vet had often pointed out on increasingly regular visits, finding a home for a geriatric poodle with dementia would be a tough task.

It was his time.

'Do you want me to take him?' the vet asked.

'Please.'

'Do you want his collar?'

'No, thank you.'

He shook the vet's hand and thanked him, saw him out, and then spent ten minutes trying to find where Rita kept the bin liners. Walking around the apartment, he filled it with Pepper's things, kneeling and checking under the bed, in the laundry, under the sofa, making sure that every last thing of his was gone, then throwing the bag down the chute. Annoyed at the dog hair on his favourite suit, he stripped it off and changed, then threw his suit down the chute too.

Only when every last trace of Pepper was gone did Luca head back to the office.

CHAPTER THIRTEEN

'I'M SURE I'm pregnant,' Evelyn said firmly. If she said it assuredly enough then the universe wouldn't dare to argue.

'Let's just wait and see what the clinic says.' Emma attempted caution. 'You'll know tomorrow.'

'I've got all the symptoms,' Evelyn insisted. 'I mean, I feel sick all the time, my breasts are hurting…' It was like water torture—drip by drip, Evelyn listed her symptoms, each one causing a further stab of unease in Emma. 'I just want to know *now*.'

So too did Emma.

'Evelyn…' Emma picked up her bag. 'I'm going out for my lunch break, okay?'

'Out?' Evelyn frowned, as well she might.

There was no such thing as a lunch break—it was either out with Luca and taking notes or a quick sandwich at the desk. The requisite lunch break in this place was non-existent. 'I've got some things I need to do…' Emma slung her bag over her shoulder '…and I doubt I'll be out of here by five.'

The public toilets in a department store wasn't the best place to find out the news, but somehow she needed to be away from Luca for this. Leaning against the wall, the short wait was interminable. Picking up the indicator, she stared at it, not trying to work out the hows or whys, as the internet had already told her that—new job, lots of travel, different time zones… She had been vigilant taking her Pill but sometimes, apparently, these things happened. Picking up the instruction leaflet, she didn't need to check it as the answer was perfectly clear—whether or not it was to her liking was another matter entirely.

She walked back to work, her heart in her mouth, not even attempting to fathom Luca's reaction to the news—she was having enough trouble fathoming her own!

'Where the hell have you been?'

Luca was not in the best of moods—in fact, he hadn't been in the best of moods for a long time. Since his return from Sicily the pretence of business as usual had soon worn thin, but since Pepper's death his mood had darkened further. Still, as she slipped off her jacket his harsh tone had no impact on Emma.

'I asked where you'd been,' Luca said. 'I've been ringing your mobile.'

'At lunch,' Emma said, 'and I forgot to charge my phone.'

'You went to lunch *two hours* ago.'

'And I stayed here till eleven p.m. last night,' Emma retorted, her head too full of the sudden news to feel threatened by Luca's tone.

Maybe she should just tell him now. *Oh, I just took a pregnancy test and was building up to giving you the happy news!*

God, men had it easy at times.

She looked up at him, at a face that had once appeared to adore her, at the stern lips that had kissed her, at the hands that had soothed her, and wondered how he could have changed so. How she could possibly ever work up the courage to tell him.

She couldn't.

So, instead of explaining herself, she peeled off her jacket and then made her way to the desk, not that her lack of response deterred him. Luca rattled off a list of orders that had even Evelyn frowning at the impossibility of it all.

But Emma just set to work, dealing with the most pressing emails and telephone calls, as Evelyn dealt with Luca.

His temper was palpable, she could hear it in the impatient buzz of her intercom, could feel it from behind the thick oak door, could see it when she knocked and entered and gave him the most recent list of figures he had demanded that she pull from thin air and that though deemed urgent were given nothing more than a cursory glance.

'And remember the midday meeting tonight,'

he called to her departing back. 'Make sure I've got all the documentation I need.'

'Midday meeting tonight?'

'With the Los Angeles office.' He bared his teeth in a sarcastic smile. 'Evelyn has to leave at six tonight, so if you want your *break*, could you take it before then?'

'I've got plans tonight.' She did have plans, important plans—like seeing a doctor and trying to work out what the hell she was going to do. 'I really need to leave.'

'Would you excuse us a moment, please, Evelyn?' His voice was dark and Emma was grateful for the sympathetic smile Evelyn gave her on the way out.

'When you were offered the position...' Each word came in clipped tones, his eyes never leaving her face as he spoke, but Emma wasn't going to take this.

'I know what you're doing!'

'When you were offered the position,' Luca said again, his voice icily calm, 'it was clearly stipulated there would be extensive travel and late nights.'

'You're trying to push me into resigning.' With every interruption, with every rise in her voice, Luca leant back further in his chair, a cruel glimmer of a smile on his lips as he calmly spoke over her.

'It was clearly outlined that the reason you were being hired,' Luca smoothly continued, 'was to lighten Evelyn's workload. I value Evelyn—'

'Unlike me,' Emma spat.

'I value *all* my staff,' Luca responded, 'but Evelyn is vital—that is why I have been so accommodating with her doctor's appointments and schedules. That is why you are here—to lighten her load so that she doesn't hand in her notice.'

'Which is what you want *me* to do?'

'Why would I want you to leave?' He was smiling now—utterly boxing her into a corner. 'If Evelyn gets good news tomorrow, we'll need you on board even more. It might even mean a promotion for you!'

He kept her at the office till ten p.m., and exhausted she fell into bed, but sleep evaded her. Her mind was a whir of scattered thoughts—that she was carrying his child was just too big and too scary to contemplate. Imagining telling him, dealing with him—telling the man who so clearly didn't want her in his life that she would be in it now for ever. Whether that meant monthly maintenance payments or access visits, there was a link now that couldn't be severed.

She lay there and wondered.

He had changed, yet so had she.

It had been like a beautiful seamless dance, and somehow she had tripped—had forgotten the rules, had tipped the scales from trusting to wary almost imperceptibly.

So she lay there, trying to pinpoint the moment it had ended, when, for Luca, the light had gone out on their relationship.

Trying not to ponder what she had done wrong.

Because she had done nothing *wrong*, Emma knew that.

It wasn't about wrong or right, or trying to

please, or bending to fit—she had known from the start it would be short-lived, that Luca, by his own clear admission, would never loan his heart to anyone for long.

She had accepted the rules of the game, had gone into it utterly prepared—and had come out of it utterly broken.

Had been so sure that she could handle it.

Change him. Be the one.

Glimpse a future for them.

So, instead of sleeping, she lay there, rueing her own carelessness, because she had been taught, and she had learnt, and yet she had chosen to forget.

What a fool she'd been…

CHAPTER FOURTEEN

THE call when it came was unexpected. Luca had won, Emma finally decided. She had her notice typed up and printed off and it sat waiting in her bag for when the right moment presented itself. She simply couldn't do it any longer.

Evelyn had had her blood test that morning and the bad news that very afternoon. Luca had offered to let her go home, but Evelyn had declined. 'This will *not* be the last time,' he had said to her, as Emma had sat with her arm around Evelyn.

'Maybe it's time to see someone else. I have found out about a very good clinic. Their success rate with IVF is high.' He handed his PA a thick glossy brochure.

'We can't afford to go there,' Evelyn sobbed.

'I am to be sent the bills,' Luca said, 'and this time you will take the time off that you need and rest properly while you wait for the results.'

'Why would you do this for me?' Evelyn wailed as Emma wondered the same thing—he could be so nice, so charming, so very, very kind. Ah, but Evelyn was vital to Luca, she thought cynically, the last thing he must privately want was for his esteemed PA to be leaving—but his show of kindness *had* caught her off guard.

As he always did.

Her throat thickened with tears as he spoke to Evelyn, as she heard again the rare tenderness that *she* craved from him. 'Because you do so much for me, because always you have been loyal to me. Because I know that when your baby is here—and it *will* be here, Evelyn—that even if you come back to work for me part time, or even if you decide to never work again, I will be able to call on you, perhaps to train someone up, perhaps to help for a few days. And more than that, we are friends. I know I can count on you, and you can count on me too.'

When he was nice, there was no one nicer, Emma realised.

No one.

Evelyn was perhaps the one woman he could sustain a relationship with because there was no sex involved, no attraction, just mutual liking and respect.

Emma would kill to have the latter two from him.

Later, sitting at her desk, staring out at the grey autumnal sky that declared summer over, when Luca strode past her desk and to his office and slammed the door behind him, she felt like one of the trees waving in the streets below. Slight, every breeze exposing the bare truth beneath, and she couldn't do it to herself any longer.

Couldn't cling on when there was nothing left—couldn't stave off winter.

She didn't hate him after all, she only hated his behaviour.

Hated it that he didn't love her.

And she must remember this, Emma realised, when she told him about the baby.

If she told him.

She let out a slow breath at the *immoral* choice she was considering taking—denying him the knowledge of the child that she was carrying.

That she *would* carry until she gave birth to it.

Oh, she would love to be one of those stoic women, one who had never considered the alternatives to giving birth—except she had. Had scoured her magazines for information, had searched on the internet, had made a couple of phone calls—and yet it was Evelyn who had unwittingly halted that thought process. Evelyn's very real grief at what had just been lost that had reminded Emma of the miracle that had occurred.

That despite precautions, despite a man who wanted nothing more than a short-lived affair, despite a woman who'd had other plans, a life had been created. A life that she would cherish for ever.

It was taking some getting used to, that was all.

She had never felt closer to understanding her mother. She finally understood now how her mother could have felt trapped inside her role of wife and mother. Hopefully, for Emma, that feeling would one day soon be diminished by the overwhelming love she would feel for her child.

Would Luca feel the same?

Tears stung her eyes as she tried to predict his likely reaction—no doubt he would assume she was just after a monthly support cheque or, even worse, a wedding ring.

Well, a loveless marriage wasn't on her agenda—she was the product of one after all and would never expose her own child to it. So now she just had to tell him, only exactly which piece of information Emma didn't know yet—that she was leaving for good or that they had created a child together.

And so busy was Emma, wrestling with her decision, that when the call came, although it was not entirely unexpected, it *was* like a bolt from the blue.

CHAPTER FIFTEEN

'SIGNORA D'AMATO. COMESTA?' Emma responded to the familiar voice in very new Italian but the greeting faded as her mind registered Luca's mother's voice, and heard the effort and emotion behind the thickly accented English when she asked if Luca was in the office.

'I'll put you through.'

'No!' Mia's voice was urgent. 'Emma, please—the news is not good.' A strangled sob from Mia had Emma closing her eyes at the raw sound of pain. 'Rico has gone.' Emma held the phone and her eyes remained closed as Mia wept for a moment before speaking again. 'I do not know Luca's reaction, they were not close, but can you tell him…gently for me?' Emma could feel the beads of sweat on her forehead, as it wasn't her job to do something so personal. Except it wasn't about her job role—Mia thought they were in love.

But only one of them was.

'I will see you both soon for the funeral.' Mia's assumption had Emma's heart pounding, and more so when she continued talking, giving Emma details that only a fiancée should know. She concluded. 'Emma, this will be hard for Luca—I am so glad that he has you.'

The walk to his office was impossibly long, yet all too soon she was there. As were her instructions, she knocked and waited for his bored voice to summon her inside.

Had he looked up, maybe he would have seen her pale face and realised something was seriously wrong, but he was deep in the middle of a phone call, his long legs on the desk and crossed at the ankles, and he waved her to sit down, which Emma did, sitting quietly, going over and over in her head how she should break it to him.

'Yes?' As he replaced the receiver he also pulled his legs from the desk and adopted a more formal position, his curt word reminding her that Luca liked to be brought straight to the point— only she truly didn't know how to just come out and say it.

'I have something to tell you.'

'So tell me.'

'It's difficult.' Emma swallowed, then opened her mouth to speak, but Luca overrode her.

'Then let me make it easy for you—you've come to hand in your notice.' He opened a drawer and handed her a thick cream envelope, his relief evident. 'I have written a reference, as we agreed—'

'Luca—'

'There will be a bonus in your pay.' Again he spoke over her. In fact, for Luca the words were tumbling out. He had known this moment was coming, had engineered it, wanted it, needed it to happen, only when the moment had arrived, it was unusually hard, painful even, and he noticed just the smallest shake to his usually steady hand as he held out the envelope. 'It is for the best,' Luca said, more for his benefit than hers.

'Luca, will you please just *listen*?' she begged, wringing her hands in her lap. 'I just took a call from your mother.' And he could hear her voice, see her mouth move, only he couldn't quite process the words, his hand still holding out the envelope as somewhere he computed that his father was dead, that finally it was over… He had wished for this moment, Luca reminded himself as something catapulted him from his seat, had him striding to the window and turning his back to Emma. He had wanted this, wished for so long that it would be over, but he had never imagined mourning, grieving. He had never considered that it actually might hurt him.

He was dead, he was gone, it was over. Finally it was over, finally he should be able to breathe, only he couldn't. He actually couldn't drag in the air or push it out, even thought he might fold over in two, because it was all there in front of him—every memory, good and bad, playing out before his closed eyes, and futile questions playing over and over like a mantra in his pounding head.

Why?

Why had his father been like that?

Why couldn't he have just been happy?

Why?

He was almost doubled over with the agony of it all—shocked at the depth of his grief over a man who had caused nothing but pain.

'When?' he asked instead.

'Just now,' Emma said gently. 'Your mother has a friend with her; she's staying in a hotel tonight and then coming home in the morning.'

He was obviously devastated, and she felt like an intruder almost, witnessing this most private moment, knowing Luca would never have chosen for her to see him like this. There were no tears, no outward, dramatic displays of emotion—they would have been easier to deal with somehow. No, it was his *pain*, this deep, wretched pain that sagged those strong shoulders as he had strode to the window then stumbled, bemused almost. She had sat there, torn—instinct wanting her to run to him, yet logic telling her to stay exactly where she was.

'And Pa?' She heard him attempt to inject strength to his voice. 'Did she say anything?'

'She asked if you could sort that out… arrange things.'

Only that wasn't what he'd meant. Everything was already sorted, things had been put in place weeks ago—all he had to do was pick up the phone, or ask Evelyn to. No, that hadn't been what he'd meant and he had never thought he would care enough to ask it.

'Did he suffer?'

'No.'

At one time he had wanted him to suffer—had wanted the agony he had inflicted to catch up with his father in death—but wishes were but flights of the imagination, Luca realised, reality entirely different.

'Your mother said it was very quick and peaceful at the end.'

That *did* give comfort, why he didn't know. And then he felt it, her hand on his shoulder, and he wanted to brush it off, ashamed at being seen like this, embarrassed that she should witness such private pain. Yet her touch helped, the bliss of human contact was like a rope to cling to in the dark, ferocious waters of grief. Luca turned and for the first time in his life and only for a moment so fleeting it was barely there he leant on another, felt her warmth, her kindness, felt *her* tears on *his* cheeks and accepted the bewildering fact that for a moment she shared his pain, divided it, lessened it even, just by being there.

And then he let her go.

Had to let her go.

'Organise the plane—I need to be there for my mother. When did you say she gets back?'

'Tomorrow, late morning.'

Which gave him space. He thought of the

billion and one things he had to do—of the people relying on him, of things he *had* to do.

'Arrange that I leave at eight a.m. tomorrow. Now, if you will excuse me, I should ring my mother.'

'Of course, but—'

'Cancel my diary for the week—I have warned most people that this might happen soon.' He was back in business mode, standing tall and proud but unable to meet her eyes.

'Luca…'

He glanced at the envelope he was still holding. 'If you were thinking of leaving, I would appreciate it if you could stay on at least till I return.'

'Of course, but…' How to say it, how to just come out and say it? Finally, the words just flurried out. 'Your mother thinks that I will be coming with you—she is expecting me to be there for the funeral.'

'No.' His response was immediate. He could not do this again, could not let her any closer, because it had already been hard enough losing her once—he couldn't do it again. 'I will explain you are needed here.'

'She thinks I am more needed there.' Emma was crying. It wasn't her place to cry, it was his father that was dead, but to see him so lost for that moment, to feel the weight of his pain momentarily rest in her arms, even if it would be agony, even if it was just another charade, she wanted to be there for him. She wanted this time with the man she loved, with the father of her child and maybe, just maybe, being with him, sharing in his grief, might bring them close enough for Emma to reveal her news. 'You don't have to do this alone.'

'No.' His response was final. He had done everything alone—always he had been alone. Oh, there had been women, so-called partners even, and they had shared in important milestones, family occasions even—yet in his mind he had always been alone. Now she offered a different path and Luca gazed into her eyes and down that unfamiliar route.

To have her with him, to get through this and

have her beside him at night, to have that hand hold his as he tried to make it through…

Never had he been more sorely tempted.

'No.'

He dismissed her, picked up the phone and turned his back.

She quietly closed the door on her way out, and she held it together.

Evelyn was still in tears for her own reasons, so with just a little guidance from her senior, Emma put the plans for Rico D'Amato in place, and for Luca D'Amato too. She struggled through the wretched day and then headed not to home but to visit her father.

'I loved her, Emma.' He was holding a photo of her mother and weeping when she arrived. 'I loved her.'

'I know, Dad.'

'I always knew she'd leave me. I knew that one day she'd go….'

Instead of taking the photo away, instead of filling up his little dish with chocolate, or replacing his laundry, Emma sat in the stiff leather chair by his bed—weary with new understanding.

Love hurt.

Love sucked.

Love made you do the unfathomable.

'I should have supported her with her art,' Frank wept, as Emma held his hand and closed her eyes. 'I should have been there for her. I should have been a better father for you…'

Round and round he went, trapped in a circle of dementia and bitter, bitter regret.

It was exhausting to listen to.

And exhausting to leave.

Bone weary, she stepped out of the nursing home and into the dark night, almost knowing Luca would be waiting for her, almost sensing what was to come.

'I went to your home.'

'I was visiting Dad.'

'We are finished, Emma.' He made himself say it, because she deserved better than lies, better than false promises.

Better than him.

'There can be no relationship.'

'I know that now.' And she did, finally she did, because he couldn't make it any clearer. His face was stripped of colour, just the blue of his eyes and the blackness of his words resonated in her heart. But love made you daft, love made you care, love made you weak at times, but true love, real love, actually made you incredibly strong.

'Your offer to come to the funeral, I would like to accept it now. It would mean a lot to my mother and also to me,' he admitted. One slight weakness and she blinked in confusion, because sometimes he sounded like a man who adored her.

'I said I'll come, but there can be no...' She couldn't finish but she knew he understood her. Unlike before, this time she meant it, because although she loved him, and wanted him, being intimate with a man who had confessed he didn't want her meant there was one rule that had to be voiced.

'I understand that,' Luca said, and he did.

Always sex had been like balm, a release, a distraction, a pleasure—yet with Emma it had been something else, had taken him to places that had shown him all he was missing, all he must forever miss. Emma had been right too. His mother had naturally assumed Emma would join him, and at first he had reeled from even the thought. But to have her beside him… He knew he shouldn't but, selfishly, his need overrode logic.

'I am leaving in the afternoon now—Evelyn will come to your home in the morning to assist you.'

And in Luca's world no explanation was necessary—he could just give his orders and they would be followed. But as Evelyn arrived the next morning with an array of dour suits, as she helped her junior pack and pay last-minute bills and cancel plans and ring the nursing home, the mood was sombre. Black was Emma's safe staple—a suit, a jumper, a sexy little dress—but always it was lightened with colour. Pulling on black stockings, a thin black cashmere jumper and then the black suit, Emma felt sick. She had never been to a funeral before—well, just one, but she had been too young to remember her mother's.

They sat in silence in Emma's lounge, waiting for the toot of Luca's driver. Evelyn saw her junior's pinched face and restless foot that tapped a silent tune as she braced herself for whatever lay ahead.

'I know something happened in Italy,' the older woman said gently.

'How could it not have?' Emma gave a tight shrug.

'I warned you,' Evelyn said, but there was no accusatory note in her voice. She had seen it before and she would no doubt see it again—but it felt different with Emma. 'You don't have to go to this—'

'But I do,' Emma interjected.

'He'll hurt you,' Evelyn warned. 'Please don't get too involved... Luca's incapable of commitment.'

'I know that.'

'And he can't stand to look at his mistakes.' Evelyn spoke from years of experience. 'I've seen it happen so many times. Sooner or later, you'll end up leaving. Oh, you'll get a glowing reference, a fabulous payout…' Each word was like an arrow to Emma's heart, because it washed away the last dregs of the uniqueness that she'd been sure had been them. 'He'll hurt you,' Evelyn said again and then the car tooted its summons and they both stood, Emma tempted to follow Evelyn's advice—to just walk away now, before he hurt her even further.

'He already has,' Emma admitted finally.

'Then tell him you can't go with him, tell him that you've changed your mind.'

The doorbell rang and the two women stood in silence for a moment, but then Emma picked up her bag and opened the door. She stared into navy eyes that were glassy, and saw a taut, guarded face that, for a little while longer at least, needed her there.

Real love *did* make you strong, Emma realised.

It wasn't just for Luca she would go to the funeral.

It was for their baby. For the little bit of history that she would one day have to repeat to their child whose grandfather had just died.

CHAPTER SIXTEEN

EVERYTHING seemed different. As the helicopter swept them from the airport, Emma could see the bare vines and naked trees and as they made their way towards Luca's home, the Mediterranean pulsing swollen and grey as they came in closer to land.

They walked into the house. All the curtains were drawn and a wail went up, women dressed in black sobbing as Luca and Emma entered.

She had never seen such raw emotion and it made her flinch—this wall of pain that hit them with force. In the middle of them all was Mia, who sat dignified and silent. She stood as her son entered and accepted his embrace, and suddenly Emma experienced a stirring of memory within her. Tears and black and grief… She could remember holding her hands up to her father, who didn't notice, could feel again the bemusement she had felt as a child, seeing her brothers weep, her aunts, everyone… Emma had been holding Luca's hand for appearances' sake but suddenly he was holding hers.

Mia led them both past the kitchen where the men stood in strained, respectful silence and into Rico's study, where she spoke with her son about the arrangements. But despite what was expected of them, Luca put his foot down. For his mother he would do it, would stand in the kitchen with the men and drink whisky and play the dutiful son, would put himself through whatever was expected of him this one last time, but he would not do it to Emma.

'Luca!' She could hear his mother's annoyance, and had no idea what they were saying, but Luca seemed adamant, his voice, firm and non-negotiable, then he led her away, up to the bedroom, where she sat on the edge of the bed.

'What was all that about?' Emma asked. 'Surely now is not the time to argue with your mother?'

'You are expected to sit and weep with the women while I stand with the men.' He watched her eyes widen in horror. 'So, perhaps now *is* a good time to state my opinion, hmm?'

'Yes, thank you,' she conceded. 'What did you say?'

'That you are tired, upset…' He gave a thin smile. 'That you are English.'

Emma managed a watery smile back. 'We English have emotions too, you know.'

'Ah, but you hide them so well.' She was quite sure he was talking about them, about these past hellish weeks. 'When it hurts, when it really hurts…' His hand reached out, pushed a few stray curls back from her strained face and he just stood there, his hand resting on the side of her cheek as her skin warmed to his slight touch. 'You just keep it all in.'

'Crying and screaming doesn't change anything. I learnt that long ago.'

'You just get on with it?' he wanted to know.

'Yes.'

'Maybe living in England, some of your ways have rubbed off on me.'

She felt as if he was giving her a message, as if beneath his blandness, beneath the void of emotion there was a deeper meaning in his words—which was the edge of madness, Emma reasoned. There was no deeper meaning with Luca, he had told her that from the start, so she jerked her head, removed herself from his contact and wished him gone.

'I must go back down, I will bring you some supper.'

'I'm not hungry,' she told him.

He didn't listen, and returned a few minutes later with a plate of pastries and a large mug of hot chocolate and some liquor. 'My mother said to give you this—it's limoncello—made from the lemons from the family tree, it will help you rest.' He poured her a small glass and Emma took it, but placed it on the bedside table.

'I should join them,' he said.

'Go,' Emma replied.

'Thank you.' He stood at the door, then turned and added, 'For being here. It helps.'

'Does it?' Her eyes searched his. 'Luca, if me being here helps…' She watched his face immediately become shuttered, and knew now wasn't the time to demand answers—to ask why he shut her out over and over again, only to occasionally let her in, why he was so closed off to emotion.

'Rest,' Luca said instead, and once he had gone back to join his family, Emma undressed, feeling exhausted. Even if she weren't pregnant she wouldn't have drunk the limoncello, so she tipped the brew down the sink, hating his father's legacy. Then she undressed for bed, catching sight of herself in the mirror and noticing the slight changes in her body already. There was no bump, it was way too soon for that, but there was a softness to her belly and pressing her fingers to her pubic bone she could feel the firm wedge of muscle. Her breasts were rounder, the areolae darker—small, subtle changes that Luca would never notice. Not that he would see them because she pulled on her shapeless candy-striped flannelette pyjamas as if they were some sort of chastity belt—usually worn for a girls' movie night and certainly not seduction material.

She slipped between the crisp cotton sheets and willed sleep to come, wished it was morning and that this long night was over.

He came to bed before midnight, undressed and climbed in beside her. Silence would have been welcome, but wails of tears still filled the house at times.

'I hate this,' Luca admitted to the darkness, knowing she was awake beside him.

'I know.'

'This day has been coming for a long time.'

'You can never prepare for losing someone you love.'

'I don't love him.' She lay still beside him, her heart stopping for a moment as she heard his truth. 'I have *never* loved him.'

'Luca…' She shook her head on the pillow. 'You shouldn't speak like that on the eve—'

'So he is a saint now?' She heard the flash of anger in his voice. 'All those people out there think they are mourning a good man, a loving husband, a wonderful father, when the truth is…' He halted, but Emma wouldn't let him leave it.

'What *is* the truth, Luca? How bad was it?'

'He beat her.' Here in the dark, with her hand slipping into his, he said it. 'Over and over he beat her, yet she never cried, she just took it. Only even if she made no noise, you could still hear it…' The marrow chilled in her bones as he continued. 'Of course, we were not allowed to tell, of course Ma covered her bruises.'

'What was he like…' Emma swallowed '…to you and Daniela?'

'Daniela was his angel—people say children know, but I am not sure as Ma and I hid it well, even from her.'

'And you?'

He didn't answer, so she asked again, her hand

reaching out to the scar on his cheek, and he held her hand against it for a moment.

'Did he do this?'

He didn't say anything more and it took a moment for Emma to realise that he was finally asleep—exhaustion catching up with him at last.

He reached for her in sleep, one strong arm dragging her that little bit closer, and she lay rigid in his arms, telling herself to pull away, except she had never felt closer to him, remembering his tension when they'd lain here all those weeks ago, when every noise, every creak of the house must for Luca have screamed danger.

Sleep didn't let him rest quietly, though.

With every noise she felt the slight jump of muscle still loaded with adrenaline, his arms pulling her further in until she could feel the press of his groin against hers.

She could feel the hardness of his erection, the tense heat of him, a need so demanding it must have woken him, because he turned away, moved onto his back, remembering their rules.

But distance didn't help it abate.

She knew that, could feel the thick energy in the room, could hear his tense breathing as he willed it to pass, for sleep to rescue him. For this hell to be over.

She turned on her side, and as her eyes adjusted to the darkness, she could see his were closed, could see the muscled outline of his stomach and the sheet that didn't disguise his need in the slightest.

Her hand reached out, resting on his stomach, and she heard his hiss of frustration as he thought inadvertent contact had been made, knew he assumed her asleep beside him—that, like himself, her body had forgotten the rules.

Well, it hadn't.

Slowly she traced the line of hair that snaked from his umbilicus, then nervous, tentative but bold she touched him, hearing his moan, running her finger along a thick vein, then tracing the path back, then doing it again.

'Emma…'

'Shh…' She didn't want questions and she didn't want answers. She was stroking him more firmly now, and then his hand was over hers.

'You don't have to…'

'I *want* to.'

'Why?'

Because she loved him, because she wanted him, because always, always she would—and despite her promises to herself, she could never lie in a bed beside him and not want him.

And because he needed this—in the thick of night, for Emma it really was that simple.

So she kissed him.

Kissed him in a place she'd never once have considered.

Licked his lovely length so slowly it took for ever to get to the top as he moaned again.

The dark made her brave, braver with each kiss, with each stroke of her tongue. She could feel his fingers in her hair now, guiding her, hear his breath quicken, her hair a thick curtain around his centre, shielding her from the world, to a place where she could just be, where it was just them and she could focus only on this. It was an act of pure giving and it came from the heart with no hope of return. She was crying when he climaxed, her salt mingling with his as he shuddered his release.

He pulled her up to his arms, and he held her, he spooned right into her and held her close and then he asked, 'Why would you do that for me?'

Only Emma didn't reply. She could feel him unwound and relaxed beside her now, felt his breath even out as he drifted into decent sleep. She knew her answer.

But it wasn't for Luca to hear.

She was embarrassed.

He was pretending to be asleep when she awoke, deliberately ignoring her—and Emma lay next to him for a moment, her body one burning blush as she remembered last night and the intimacy she had bestowed on a man who had so clearly told her this was for appearances' sake only.

Quietly she slipped from the bed and walked to the en suite, closing the door behind her, then sitting on the edge of the bath and resting her burning face in her hands.

She should never have agreed to this, should never have come back to Italy. Even if she had convinced herself that it was for all the right reasons—for Mia, to keep up appearances, for Luca even—in part, a very big part, it had been for her, for some time with him, for that chance to rekindle or reawaken in Luca some of the feelings that had once existed.

Instead, thanks to his silence this morning, she had found out what she had always known.

It was sex he wanted from her—and nothing more.

She showered, wishing the water could wash away her shame, her stupidity. She, Emma Stephenson, had been so sure she could handle it, so sure she would never succumb to his fatal charms. Eventually, like all the rest, she had. Bit by bit, each rule, each guideline had been chipped away—each time she had promised herself that this would be the last…

Till next time.

Turning off the shower, she shivered and reached for a towel that wasn't there. Walking across the bathroom, she stood naked as he walked in, her hands moving to cover herself as she leant against the sink.

'Don't you ever knock?' She attempted a smile to save face, and hoped the steam and the water from the shower would hide the evidence of her tears.

But he saw her.

Saw the body he had missed for weeks and saw the changes too.

Full, ripe breasts made his throat catch, and he noticed the dusting of weight on her hips, although there was something else too that he couldn't define, an added dimension to her femininity.

She was like a drug that kept beckoning. Never had he cared for someone like this before—last night he had accepted the release she had offered, not for escape but to go back, to return, to savour the feelings they had once created in one another.

He had told her some of it, he had told her, and she hadn't blanched or turned away from his horrible past—and he was finally glimpsing a future, a future where bathroom doors were open, where you kissed and made up and you tried again.

Where you were there for each other.

'Why would I knock?' he teased gently.

'Because…' She was starting to cry and couldn't help it. 'Because…'

He pressed her against the sink with his kiss—naked, gorgeous, she made today possible. He had sworn to never again make love with her, he had sworn to just let her go, let her be, keep her safe, but he was finally seeing things differently.

She was safer by his side.

Safer with him than without him.

He kissed her as if it was the first time, relishing her all over again.

'You do make things better. With you things are better.' And that he remembered their words, that each conversation they'd ever had was in his head the same way it was in hers, brought assurance. 'You could *always* make things better...'

'This isn't just sex.' She wept out the words as he lifted her to the edge of the sink. His mouth lowered and suckled her swollen breast as her fingers knotted in his hair.

'No,' he murmured, because it wasn't. This was it, this was him and this was her and this was the place he always wanted to be. He lifted his head and kissed away her tears, kissed her mouth as his hands followed the curve of her thickening waist.

'Don't hurt me again, Luca...' she begged brokenly.

His eyes jerked up to hers, his mouth pulling away simultaneously with her words. Was that what he had done? Yes, he acknowledged. In protecting her, he had hurt her badly.

He could never hurt her again, never would

hurt her again. Of that, at this very moment, he was absolutely certain.

'Never.' He growled out his truth.

'And tell me this isn't just sex,' she pleaded as his hips parted her thighs, because it wasn't just sex for her, because she could never be so real, so open, so exposed with anyone other than Luca. His fingers spread her pretty butterfly lips and he saw changes there too, and he was awash with this fierce surge of protection, assured in his answer.

'No.' His mouth was in her neck, he was as close to weeping as he had ever been. Her curls, wet from the shower, draped his face and as he slid inside her, he was certain of the moment. He was smelling her again, tasting her again, inside her again, and he was truly home, deep, deep inside her. His arms circled her, his mind wrapped around hers, and this was nothing like anything he had ever envisaged. Then she was arching towards him and he didn't have to hold back, he didn't have to do anything except love her, and that was so scarily easy.

The passion that blazed in his eyes should have assured her, but then he lowered his head. Nuzzling her shoulders, her neck, he drove deeper into her, only she couldn't give in, couldn't let herself be swept away by the building current, because she couldn't risk going under again.

Her body was twitching, her legs wet and wrapped around him, and it was Emma who sought release now. She could see his jet curls, see him slide in and out of her, and knew he was ready, knew he awaited her—but she was too scared to trust, too scared to hand over that last little bit of her heart to him.

She wanted his love, wanted a father for her baby, wanted him no matter how her head denied it.

She knew he was close and, locked into a rhythm, his body begged her to join him. He was saying her name over and over, his lips kissing the back of her neck, his hands cupping her damp bottom, and she could feel his abandon.

'*I love you.*' He groaned out the words as if it

hurt to say them. She'd never thought she'd ever hear him say them, but he was saying them again and again, saying them over and over as he spilled inside her, rapid, urgent thrusts that took her to this heady place where she gave in to him, gave in to her body, and she was saying it too.

He was kissing her passionately, his tongue circling hers, as finally she joined him, and he dragged from her that last restraint. His mouth stifled her sobs as she gave that piece to him and then his tongue soothed her as he slowly kissed her back to the world.

'You,' Luca said slowly, wrapping a towel around her, holding her shivering body, comforting her on a day when it should be her comforting him, 'make this day bearable.'

CHAPTER SEVENTEEN

SHE was pregnant.

Of that he was sure.

That the baby was his there was no doubt.

He stood in the church, supporting his mother, his weeping sister, and stared beyond the priest to the baptismal font. He tried to comprehend the fact of the D'Amato name carrying on after all—his baby, the future, the family name continuing.

Tried to imagine himself as a father.

Could he do it—could he break every promise he had made to himself?

Today he did his duty, threw a handful of dirt on the coffin and then stepped back.

It should be over—and yet the cycle might now continue.

His mind was a blizzard of conflicting emotions, every tombstone reminding him of his history, of his legacy, of the true meaning of his family name. He wanted to go back to this morning, to the certainty he had felt then, the assuredness that no harm would ever come to someone he loved.

The priest was talking about faith and hope and love.

His faith had long since gone.

He desperately wanted to hope.

And he was terrified to love.

But he was dangerously close to accepting a different future.

He needed to think.

'Come...' Mia was calmer. Her tears had filled the church but now she seemed resigned. 'The cars are waiting.'

'I will make my own way back.' Luca looked over at Emma. 'You go to the house.'

'You need to greet the guests,' she pointed out.

'I want to walk.'

'You must come back to the house,' Mia said in exasperation. 'As his only son, it is tradition…'

'I will be back.' Luca refused to be swayed. 'But right now I need to be alone.'

He did, he needed so badly to be alone, because this was too big to leap into without serious thought.

Soon Emma would tell him, soon he would formally know that he was to become a father, and his response had to be right.

He walked around the graveyard then stood for a pensive moment.

He could hear his mother's bitter words from the past as clearly as though she'd just said them to him. *You are no better than him—you are the same. You are a D'Amato through and through.*

'Luca!' Leo stood beside him as he stared at his father's new grave. 'Can I give you a lift back to the house?'

'I am not going back yet—I want to walk.'

'Do you mind if I join you?' He was about to decline the offer of company, only Leo was wise.

Surely, at some point over the years, he must have treated his mother's wounds or at least seen what was going on—maybe the older man could give him answers.

They walked in silence—through the winding roads and to the next village, where finally they sat. Luca ordered coffee and whisky and wondered how to ask without telling.

'Emma seems a lovely woman.' Leo broke the silence.

'She is,' Luca agreed.

'It is good to see you two supporting each other, Luca. To know even in sad times you can find peace.'

'Can I speak with you as a doctor?' Luca asked bluntly.

'Of course.'

'I think she may be pregnant,' he revealed. The doctor didn't offer congratulations; instead he waited to hear what else Luca had to say. 'I have questions, Leo. Things I need to know about my past, about me…'

'Then ask,' Leo offered, 'and I will try to give honest answers.'

'Always I feel different from my father—my mother says I am the same, that I am like him…' He watched as Leo's drink paused near his lips. 'Do you understand what I'm saying?'

'I think so.'

'Is it true?'

'Is what true, Luca?' Leo asked.

That I will beat my wife, that the cruel streak of the D'Amato men is my inevitable fate—or Emma's? This was what he wanted to say, but instead he downed his drink.

'I should never have started this.' Luca stood up. 'I should get back to the house.'

'Sit, Luca.' Leo gestured to the waiter to fill his glass, but Luca remained standing. 'There are things we need to discuss, and it will be better for you, for Emma too perhaps, to know the truth.'

'I don't want to discuss it any more,' Luca said, because even if he had started it, he didn't want to go there, didn't want to face the inevitable, but it was coming at him now.

'There is a good counsellor in Palermo, one I highly recommend to deal with these things.'

'No!' He shouted it.

'Luca, you cannot escape your genes.' It was like hearing the guillotine fall, the truth was so appalling, and the horrible inevitability had Luca wanting to vomit. But instead he drowned the acrid taste in his mouth with whisky and willed the fear to abate as the doctor delivered his diagnosis that no matter the strength of Luca's feelings, his unenviable gene pool would claim, not just him but Emma and the baby he was sure she carried.

'No!' It was Emma's sobs that filled the house—and Luca had to restrain her flailing arms from making contact with his chest as he broke her heart again. 'You said you *loved* me.'

'Emma.' His voice was detached, matter-of-fact even, as she raged at what he was doing, at what he was saying. 'I was upset this morning, emotional…'

'You!' Emma sobbed. '*Emotional?* You're a cold-hearted bastard. You looked me in the eyes and said you loved me, and you *did* love me, I could see it.' She wanted to lash out again if he would just let go of her arms.

'People say that…' Luca's was the voice of cool reason. 'Men say that, you know that. Men say these things to—'

'Get what they want?' Emma finished for him. 'You already *had* what you wanted, Luca. You were already screwing me when you said it!'

'Don't talk like a tart.'

'Well, that's what *you* made me, that's what *you* did to me!' And then, because he was holding her arms, because she couldn't hit him again, she swore at him instead.

And then she swore again, using the most vile epithets she could think of.

He didn't even flinch.

* * *

She didn't tell him about the baby, didn't play her last card.

And for that Luca had grudging admiration.

She didn't cash in the cheque he sent her, which made Luca worry.

In the weeks and months that followed, every day he waited, for her letter, or her lawyer's letter, or a phone call—admiring her that it never came, eroding him that it didn't.

Back in his village for another tour of duty, for the three-month mass to mark his father's passing, it killed him to be back in the same room, only this time without her.

He lay in bed that morning, not wanting to get up, not wanting to shower, to walk into the bathroom, where he had told her his ultimate truth.

He *had* hurt her.

Not in the way that he had feared, but he *had* hurt her all the same.

He had never—except in this—doubted himself.

And he was angry now.

Angry for doubting himself, because after

weeks of soul searching he knew—Luca knew—he would never hurt her. His grief on the night of his father's funeral and in the days that had followed had been real—except it had all been because of losing Emma.

Since she'd left, in the depths of his grief, this proud man *had* visited a counsellor—although not the Italian one Leo had suggested. Instead, he had sat in a bland beige office in the middle of London and had opened his closed heart to a stranger, explored his closed mind in a way he had never dared to do before, and he knew now.

Knew, despite his heritage, despite what Leo had said, despite the facts and figures, despite the anger of his youth and the unenviable history of the D'Amato men, he knew that his anger *would* never, *could* never be aimed at her.

For the very first time he trusted himself, except now it was maybe too late.

'Luca?' His mother knocked and then came into the bedroom, placed coffee on the bedside table and handed him the tray then headed to the window, opening the shutters and letting the sun stream in.

'You did not have to do that!' Luca protested. 'I should be looking after you.'

'You should be looking after Emma,' his mother pointed out.

She was dressed in black. This was a dark day, but there was a lightness to her—the absence of fear, Luca realised. Oh, she would respectfully mourn her husband, but her duty was done now, there would be no feigned tears—life could be peaceful now.

For her.

'I thought I *was* looking after her,' Luca said, 'by keeping her away. I thought I was doing the right thing by her.'

'How?' Mia begged. 'I thought you were happy with Martha, but with Emma I just knew… How could you think you were helping her by ending it? Emma loves you.'

'I did not want to be like *him*.'

'I know I said hurtful things to you, out of fear,

out of pain, out of guilt, and for that I am truly sorry. But you are *nothing* like him,' his mother said fiercely.

'I know that *now*,' Luca said. 'But I still wasn't sure back then.'

'Leo said you spoke with him.' Mia sat on the edge of the bed, her eyes sparkling with tears. 'I don't understand, Luca. He said you understood your past, and wanted to ask him about it. I know it must have been a shock, that it must have caused you pain to hear the truth, but to end it with Emma! Why, Luca?'

'Because Leo said it was in my blood, that I could not escape my genes. That the violent traits in my grandfather, my uncle, my father could not be denied. I said I felt nothing like them and he said he knew it was hard to accept, to face…'

A moan of horror escaped his mother's lips…a sound of such pain that Luca started with concern. She had always been silent, even when being beaten, but she was moaning in pain now, a pain he didn't understand, her eyes frantic and urgent and loaded with tears when they met her son's. 'To accept and face the truth that *Leo* is your real father…'

It was as if the sun had gone out. Everything suddenly went dark, as if the bed had been pulled from under him, as if the floor had just given way. Every rock, every foundation collapsed beneath him, yet he never moved, never moved a muscle, his mother's voice seeming distorted from a distance as his mind frantically tried to process the words.

'I thought you knew,' Mia pleaded. 'Leo thought that you knew, that you had finally guessed…'

As he looked back on their conversation with the knowledge the other man held, Luca closed his eyes. And as he did so, he felt the guilt, the shame, the *fear* truly unravel at last, and when he opened his eyes it was to a world that was brighter, safer. His only regret was that it was a world without Emma.

'Devo sapere,' Luca said. 'Tell me.' There was

a flash of anger then. 'Did he know, did Leo know how he was treating you?'

'Never!' Mia sobbed. 'Only you, my son, only you know my pain. I was always promised for your father—our two families were friends. I knew I would marry him, but I did not like to think about it—sixteen seemed a long way off. Always I liked Leo—he was so clever, we all knew he was destined for better and sometimes, when he came home in the holidays, I felt his eyes on me. One time we kissed...' She sighed and then visibly shook herself and continued her story.

'I worked in the baker's, my marriage was two weeks away. The village was celebrating because Leo had passed his exams and was going to study medicine in Roma; he would return a doctor. I was sad. My wedding was soon and your father had slapped me, he had pushed me, he had made me do things that shamed me...'

'He is not *my* father,' Luca corrected her, and how good those words felt!

'*Rico* had hurt me.' Mia nodded in acknowledgment. 'We closed early one day and I was walking home and I met Leo. He was leaving the next day and he said he was sorry he would not be at my wedding…then he admitted he was not sorry. That it would hurt to see me marry another. We went to the river and I nearly told him…'

'Why didn't you?' Luca asked.

'How?' Mia asked. 'Leo was a good man, even as a teenager he was a good man, a man who cared for me. He would not have gone away to get his medical degree.'

'He could have taken you with him.'

'His family would have been shamed and would not have paid for his education. After all, I was another man's bride-to-be, and this town would have never forgiven that. How, in one conversation, could I change his life when neither really knew how the other was feeling?

'We kissed, and you were made that day, Luca. It was the best day of my life, and every night I fall asleep with that memory… Yes, in hindsight

I should have told him, but we were young, and I loved him and wanted him to do well, to be happy. I would have brought him so much pain...'

'Did my fa—?' Luca stopped himself. 'Did Rico know I was not his son?'

'He never said, and sometimes I wondered if he had guessed, if that was why he was so angry with you, with me, but really he was angry with me and treated me badly before I was ever unfaithful to him.'

'And Leo?' Luca swallowed. 'When did you tell him?'

'I didn't for a long time. He was a man when he returned, and I was married with two children. He was married later too. I was friends with his wife.' The pain of her secret silenced her for a moment. 'He ended up being friends with Rico as well. No one knew the man Rico was in private. It was one time, Luca, and a long time ago, not much to ruin so many lives. When Carmella, his wife, died, Leo came over one night. He was chatting to your father and going through albums, talking of his wife, and there was a photo of you there when you got your degree. I remember him looking up at me, his eyes asking me, and I looked away, red and blushing—and from that moment he knew. He must have seen something of himself as a young man in that photo of you.'

'Have you talked to him about it?' Luca asked.

'I spoke with him a few months ago, yet we could not properly talk. He was treating Rico, his friend, but we knew we would talk one day soon.'

'And have you?'

'Soon,' Mia said. 'Still I have to break his heart by telling him all I have suffered, how you, his son, have suffered over the years.'

'How do you know it will break his heart?' he wanted to know.

'Love does not just go away, Luca.'

'I know.' He stared out the window at the Mediterranean.

'You can push it away, you can deny it, you can make excuses, give reasons, but once love has been born, once it has existed, it cannot simply cease to be.'

There were so many questions, so much more he wanted to know from his mother and from his real father, but he didn't need those answers right now.

It was Emma he needed to see and regardless of whether or not it was too late he had to tell her, which meant there was someone he had to speak with first.

'You cannot leave now,' Mia pointed out as he packed his case. 'There is mass tonight, one more duty, Luca—for *familia*…'

'No, Ma.' He kissed his mother's cheek to show he was not angry. 'My duty is to Emma—*she* is *familia* now.'

CHAPTER EIGHTEEN

'Can I pay Dad's account?'

'Of course.' The supervisor was unusually friendly as Emma came into the office, just a little bit flushed in the cheeks and, well, just a little nicer. 'You've sold another painting.'

It was actually the supervisor who handed her an envelope with a cheque in it and there was a flurry in her stomach as Emma took it. That feel of her baby moving still caught her by surprise, and she smiled, not just at the kicks from her baby but that she had almost paid her debts—and all by her own hand.

All was well.

She chanted those words over and over to herself and out loud to her baby too at times.

All was well.

Her father's house had finally sold and she'd found a little flat nearby. Thanks to an excellent reference from Luca, she'd landed a wonderful job for three days a week and once the baby arrived they were happy for her to work a couple of days a week from home, which gave her time to concentrate on her art.

She was getting there.

Not quite thriving, but not just surviving either.

She missed Luca—missed him in her days, in her nights, in her life, and she missed him for their baby too.

But there was nothing she could do about that, so she poured her grief into her artwork and scared herself sometimes with her own mind—painting dark, swirling stories of loss and grief and hope and life.

And she'd sold not one but three paintings!

She'd put one up in her father's room at the nursing home, which a relative of another resident had liked, and things had taken off from there.

Oh, they hadn't sold for vast sums, but they'd keep the baby in nappies and bottles, and Emma knew that they'd be okay.

All was well, she told her kicking stomach.

They really didn't need Luca.

Want, however, was an entirely different matter.

She walked down the long corridor towards her father and wasn't really looking forward to it. He'd noticed her swelling stomach these past couple of weeks and unfortunately a stroke and a touch of senility weren't stopping him from asking awkward questions.

Emma pulled her coat around her and held a massive photo album over her stomach, hoping a few pictures from the past would be enough to distract him.

And then she saw him.

Saw six feet two with eyes of blue, sitting chatting on the bed and laughing with her dad, and she absolutely, completely didn't know what to do.

'Here's my baby girl!' Frank beamed as she made her way over.

She kissed her dad on the cheek and ignored Luca.

He watched as she put her father's pyjamas away and sorted out his chocolate and put some money in a little dish for his newspaper—and he saw the swell of her stomach and the strain on her features, and finally, finally she faced him.

'Could we have a word?' Emma said. 'Outside.'

They walked out to the nursing-home gardens, along the winding paths, and finally she spoke.

'Don't…' Her voice was shaky. 'Don't you *dare* drag him into this! He's old and he's confused.'

'He's our child's grandfather,' Luca pointed out. 'I'd say he's already in this…and he knows, by the way.'

'Knows what?'

'That you're pregnant,' Luca said, and watched her cheeks burn. 'Were you ever going to tell me?'

'I don't know,' she said honestly.

'You don't *know*?' he repeated incredulously.

So she turned to him and just said it, too tired, too confused and too angry for his mind games this time.

'You knew anyway,' Emma accused. 'You *knew* that morning you said you loved me, and you knew it when you chose to let me go.' And it was agony when he nodded. 'So don't play the wounded party now—you chose not to be around, Luca. I *bore* you, remember?'

'Never,' Luca said, his face pale.

'And I'm *not very interesting* in bed.'

'That's not true either,' he said. How he hated hearing it, how he hated what he had done to her—and yet now he had to face it. 'All I think about is you. All I want is you—if you will give me this chance,' he vowed.

'Why would I?' She had loved him so much and he hadn't wanted that love. She could almost forgive him for herself, but she wouldn't be careless with her baby's heart. 'Why would I risk it again? We'll do fine without you.'

And she would, he knew that she would, but

how he wanted her to do better than fine—with him by her side.

'I was scared I was like my father,' he admitted.

'Not good enough, Luca.' She turned her face away. 'I'm scared I'm like my mother—but deep down I know I'll never walk away. You did.'

'He beat her.' Luca closed his eyes. 'Badly, over and over.'

'I know that,' Emma pointed out. 'And I know you never would do that to me or our baby, so why couldn't you trust that?'

'My grandfather, my uncle, they were the same too. Emma, I didn't want to hurt you.'

'But you *did*!' She was trying not to cry, trying not to get upset, trying to stay calm for the baby, but it was hard. 'Over and over you did. It doesn't have to be a fist to hurt, Luca.'

Her words sliced his heart—bitter, bitter was his regret.

'My grandmother slipped and fell.' Luca's voice was a hoarse whisper, voicing dark thoughts that had never been said. 'That is what

I was told, that was what I believed—I heard my mother sob one night that Rico was just like *his* father. "And look where my mother ended up" was Rico's response.'

It wasn't just his father, Emma started to see that now, and it wasn't just the beating…

'He killed her.'

'Oh, Luca,' Emma whispered.

'And Rico's brother, Rinaldo.' His voice was hoarse, the filth of the past all spewing out now. 'He beat Zia Maria too. Daniela remembers her as glamorous, always wearing make-up—only, of course, it was to cover the bruises.'

Emma closed her eyes, recalling the well made-up face of Rinaldo's second bride.

'Maria came to our door one night, scared and crying, yet my mother sent her away—and she was dead the next morning. Kicked by a horse, my father, the policeman, announced after he'd *investigated*.

'I grew up with this secret—a secret so well hidden that not even the family doctor could see.

My father was the trusted village policeman and yet in his home he did terrible things—his brothers and father too. And when I was younger, I promised I would never get so involved with a woman that I would marry her, give her children…' It was so hard to explain and yet he persevered. 'I thought there was this…inevitability, that the violence was in my blood, in my genes. That I had been passed not just the family name…' His eyes searched the gorgeous mound of her stomach. 'And I thought that I had passed it on too—and that the baby would have a better chance of a normal life with just you to look after it.'

'You should have told me all this,' Emma said.

'When?' Luca challenged. 'I don't come with a government warning. I made my choice to never get too involved with anyone, and then you came along and that simple resolution…' He swallowed as he recalled just how hard it had been to keep it in and how scared he had been to let it out. 'I was going to tell you. The day of the funeral, I knew somehow that I would do better, that I could not hurt you. For the first time I realised I had choices—and I also realised you had to make your choices too. It is not an easy family to marry into.'

'Marry?' Emma blinked. 'You were thinking of asking me to *marry* you that day?'

'And every day from the moment I met you—even if I didn't want to admit it,' Luca said truthfully.

'So why didn't you?' she wanted to know.

'I spoke with Leo.'

'The doctor?'

Luca nodded. 'I tried to tell him my concerns, I wanted him to reassure me, and instead he said that I could not hide from my genes. He offered me counselling. I thought he was talking about anger management…'

'How dare he?' It was Emma who needed anger management now. 'How bloody archaic, how dare he imply that you'd be like that too?'

'No.' He hushed her. 'Emma, I woke up this morning and I knew, no matter what he'd said, no matter what history dictates, that I would never, ever hurt you.'

'I knew that already,' she said, but she did understand because there was a part of her that had the same sort of fears—that she'd be a lousy mother, that she'd turn forty and some strange force would take over and she'd suddenly walk out on her family. Luca's words had rung that bell of fear that she'd heard many times before—that there was a certain inevitability to it all. 'I feel the same sometimes,' she admitted, 'that I won't be a good mum…'

'You'll be a *wonderful* mum,' he said with absolute conviction.

'You'll be a wonderful dad.'

'If you'll let me be,' he murmured.

'I could never stop that, and I know in the end I'd have told you,' she admitted.

He ran a hand over her swollen stomach, rued the moments he'd already missed and promised himself that he'd miss not a moment more.

'You're nothing like your dad,' Emma continued. 'You're like Pepper!' How she made him smile! 'Snapping and snarling, but you'd never bite. Luca…' She said it with absolute conviction. 'You're nothing like him.'

'Actually, I am *nothing* like him.'

'I just said that.'

'No…' He blew out a breath, because in all that had happened he hadn't even had time to really process the news, to even think about it, to explore it, so when he did that for the first time, he did it with her.

'I'm nothing like Rico because Leo is my real father.'

'Leo?' Emma gasped. 'The doctor, the one who said…?' She *had* thought him familiar when they'd met, and now she knew why! That assuredness, that arrogance that Luca possessed had to have come from somewhere—and now she knew where!

'That is what he was trying to say, about genes. He thought I had guessed, thought I was trying to tell him I knew. Guilt made my mother stay with Rico—and shame. Not just at what others might think but because of what she secretly knew—that she'd been unfaithful to my father even before she'd married him.'

Emma blinked in amazement, trying to take it all in.

'I love you.' And it was a different way he said it this time. Not something he dragged from himself, not something he didn't want to admit. Instead, he told her his truth. 'People make mistakes. I have just sat and listened to your father's regret about your mother and you—and I've heard my own mother's regret and guilt too. People bury their shame and fears in the past but they don't go away, they fester.' He smiled. 'Also, I have something else to tell you. Your father is not senile.' Luca gazed down at her. 'He told me that today. He knows you think he is, but his truth is that he remembers your mother now with love, and better still…' He looked at her kind, clear eyes that had never been loved and vowed to make up for all past hurts. 'Your father says he now has a second chance to love you.'

'He said that?' she choked.

'Yes.'

'He's not confused from the stroke?'

'No.' Luca grinned, the old Luca, the funny Luca, the Luca who had first won her heart. 'He's just a bit uninhibited,' Luca said, and then he was serious. 'And so now must I be.' He stared beyond her eyes and to her soul. 'I love you, Emma. I always have and I always will. I sat on the sofa that first night we met, after I came in from Paris, and there was a part of me imagining watching that detective show with you.'

He watched a pink flush warm her cheeks.

'When I left my flat for Tokyo that day, I imagined coming home to you.'

He watched as the colour spread to her little ears, saw the smile wobble on her lips, and so he told her some more.

'When you held my hand on the plane, I imagined lying next to you every night for the rest of my life.'

She could feel it, the warm glow of his love

warming her icy veins, chasing away all the hurt, the fear, the loneliness—bathing her in this deep, rosy warmth and wrapping her in soft, infinite understanding.

'You can,' Emma said, her eyes open, staring into the eyes of a man who had made it so very difficult for her to love him. 'Every night for the rest of your life, you can lie beside me.'

'You too,' Luca said, because it was such a nice thing to know, such a nice thing to be told. 'Always, I am here for you.'

And he would be, Emma knew that. Luca was here, for her, for their baby—and finally, finally she had the family she had always longed for.

'Come on,' she whispered. 'Let's go and tell Dad.'

EPILOGUE

'ONE more push,' Luca implored—as if it were that easy, as if he knew how it should be done just because he'd read it in a magazine!

'I can't!'

It wasn't pushing that scared her, it was life, because in a moment the future would be here—and although she couldn't wait to meet it, she was scared she wasn't up to it.

That, by not having grown up with a mother, she might not be able to *be* a mother herself.

It wasn't one more push, it was four, and then this wait, this rush as a bundle of red was on her stomach and Luca was cutting the cord, was over. Ready or not, she was officially a mum, so she had no choice but to be able.

'A girl!' It was the doctor who spoke because Luca just stood, his face unreadable, watching his wife reach for their daughter, watching eyes peer at a very new, very big world.

He had hoped for a boy—not for the old reasons, not for a son or to continue the family name, which was a bit of a black joke between them. No, Luca had wanted a boy because Emma was so scared of having a girl.

And as he stared at this tiny little lady, so new and so raw and so fragile, he understood her fears—because he had them too. Their daughter was surely the most precious thing in the world and they had to do this right.

'A girl…' He picked up his daughter and cradled her close, hushed angry, startled cries and then, when he was sure Emma was ready, he handed her to her mother, and he watched nature unfold, and Emma feed her hungry baby.

Watched his wife become a mother to his daughter.

The midwife tidied up around them then

opened the curtains on the beginning of a glorious new day, pinks and oranges and pretty lemons filling the window as if the sky had known it was giving her a girl.

'What a beautiful morning to become a mum!' the midwife said, and left the new family to it. Emma wanted to call her back, worried almost that she'd been left with her baby, that she should know what to do. What if she stopped feeding, or what if she suddenly cried?

But she was still feeding, making little snuffly noises as Emma stared down.

Girls were different.

Politically correct or not, scientifically based or whatever, in a hormonal haze Emma knew that they just were.

They needed cuddles and blankets and something else—something Emma had been denied and something she swore her daughter would never be without.

'If something were to happen to me...' Seeing her cradling their daughter, hearing the wobble in her voice, it would have been so easy to wave her fears away, but Luca wouldn't do that to her.

'There would be Daniela, my mother, Evelyn and her twin girls when they come… She'd be surrounded.' Luca stared at his daughter. 'But more than that, she would know about you and know how much I loved you and how much I love her.'

He left no room for doubt.

'What happened to my playboy?' she teased.

'He stopped playing.'

'What happens now?' Emma asked, because she had it all, here in this room. Here in her arms she had it all, and she didn't know quite what to do with it.

'We name her?' Luca smiled. 'Do you want to call her after your mother?'

She had thought about it long and hard and she thought about it again.

'No,' Emma admitted, because sometimes it still hurt. 'Do you want to name her after yours?'

'No,' Luca said. He had forgiven Mia, and he was happy to see her with Leo, but, well, it was all too new and too much just yet. He didn't even know what to do with his own surname, let alone pass on his mother's first name too!

'Aurora,' Emma said.

'Aurora?' Luca played with the word in his mind and liked it. 'It means dawn...'

'And new beginnings,' Emma said, gazing from her infant to her husband. They would follow their own course now. This precious clean slate they had been given deserved the very best they could give her, and that's what she would get.

A new beginning.

0410 Rom LP

MILLS & BOON PUBLISH EIGHT LARGE PRINT TITLES A MONTH. THESE ARE THE EIGHT TITLES FOR MAY 2010.

RUTHLESS MAGNATE, CONVENIENT WIFE
Lynne Graham

THE PRINCE'S CHAMBERMAID
Sharon Kendrick

THE VIRGIN AND HIS MAJESTY
Robyn Donald

INNOCENT SECRETARY...
ACCIDENTALLY PREGNANT
Carol Marinelli

THE GIRL FROM HONEYSUCKLE FARM
Jessica Steele

ONE DANCE WITH THE COWBOY
Donna Alward

THE DAREDEVIL TYCOON
Barbara McMahon

HIRED: SASSY ASSISTANT
Nina Harrington

0510 Rom LP

MILLS & BOON PUBLISH EIGHT LARGE PRINT TITLES A MONTH. THESE ARE THE EIGHT TITLES FOR JUNE 2010.

ℭ

THE WEALTHY GREEK'S CONTRACT WIFE
Penny Jordan

THE INNOCENT'S SURRENDER
Sara Craven

CASTELLANO'S MISTRESS OF REVENGE
Melanie Milburne

THE ITALIAN'S ONE-NIGHT LOVE-CHILD
Cathy Williams

CINDERELLA ON HIS DOORSTEP
Rebecca Winters

ACCIDENTALLY EXPECTING!
Lucy Gordon

LIGHTS, CAMERA...KISS THE BOSS
Nikki Logan

AUSTRALIAN BOSS: DIAMOND RING
Jennie Adams